A Tittle-Tattle Town

Published by Brolga Publishing Pty Ltd
ABN 46 063 962 443
PO Box 12544
A'Beckett St
Melbourne, VIC, 8006
Australia

email: markzocchi@brolgapublishing.com.au

National Library of Australia
Cataloguing-in-Publication data
Wyke, Fred, author.
A Tittle-Tattle Town
ISBN: 9781922175960 (paperback)
Subjects: Secrets--Fiction.
Love stories, Australian
A823.4
Printed in Australia
Cover design by Brolga Publishing
Cover image from www.freeimages.com (Artist: Dany Sabadini)
Typesetting by Tara Wyllie

BE PUBLISHED

Publish through a successful publisher. National distribution, Macmillan & International distribution to the United Kingdom, North America. Sales Representation to South East Asia
Email: markzocchi@brolgapublishing.com.au

A Tittle-Tattle Town

Fred Wyke

Foreword

Ilma Mathews has reached a cross roads in her life. Until the arrival into her small country town of the much younger Rod Skapleson, she has lived a well ordered if uninspiring life. She is the unblemished wife of Vincent Mathews, who is Headmaster of the local Primary School, a valued and respected community leader, indeed, a stalwart of the Sandhaven Creek community. But like Emma in Flaubert's *Madame Bovary*, Ilma recklessly reaches out and savours the forbidden fruits that Rod is willing to offer. Blind to the consequences she leaps into an affair of her own making. A small town is not the place for imprudent behaviour, and Ilma has become so infatuated that a sense of discretion deserts her with dire consequences.

In his first novel, Fred Wyke has conjured up an intriguing plot peopled with characters that pose uneasy questions about human motives.

Jane Kelly

Acknowledgements

The first manuscript draft for this novel was hand written, and then, at the age of eighty, I discovered the computer. I wish to thank Sue Beard at Text Management for typing and thoroughly proof reading that first manuscript, and for her assistance in getting it onto my computer.

I also wish to thank my daughter Fiona Hough and my daughter in law Jenny Wyke for their many prompt responses to my numerous telephone calls for help whenever my computer turned nasty.

My final thank you is to Jane Kelly who offered encouraging comment and wrote the forward appearing at the start of these pages.

Fred Wyke

Author's Note

The townships of Sandhaven Creek, and Dareboolah are fictional towns.

The Author has spent no more than a few hours in Tamworth and has never visited it's race track.

All of the characters and places described in this novel are drawn from the Authors imagination.

Fred Wyke

1
Ilma & Rod

Making news, Saturday 15 February 1997:
Fourteen year old Tara Lipinski has been crowned America's youngest ever figure-skating champion. She will compete in the world championships in Switzerland next month.

Comment:
There was no ice rink in the township of Sandhaven Creek, and Tara's feat was unlikely to attract the attention of any of its citizens. It was almost certain nobody in the town would be awaiting news of her progress in Switzerland. The temperature in town on this day was 34 degrees.

Sandhaven Creek, a small Australian country town, nestled in a remote valley some five hundred kilometres from the nearest state capital. Most of its residents were born and brought up in the township. They lived an insular life and knew much of each other's business.

Ilma, one of Sandhaven Creek's residents, was in an unusual state of excitement. Her normally well ordered existence had developed a flutter. No longer could she move through her daily activities in the smooth way in which she was accustomed. Her mind kept straying into the dangerous territory of romance, desire and seduction.

A place she last visited nearly fifteen years previously when for a brief time at university, she fell for the charms of Maximilian Rodda, her college fencing master – an audacious man blessed with the most lissom body she had ever seen. Ilma had bought a fencing foil and spent many enthusiastic hours in his fencing studio. She also spent several hopeful ones in his bed. But his heart was as impenetrable as his fencing guard and his interest in her soon died.

Ilma, happily married until recently, and still not unhappily so, had nevertheless been shaken out of her emotional comfort zone. A newcomer had arrived in the township, and though much younger than she, he had an uncanny resemblance to the Maximilian Rodda of her earlier memories.

In the beginning she almost bumped into this stranger when leaving the Post Office, then saw him a few times walking in the main street or around the shops. Soon she found herself spending more than her usual amount of time visiting the shopping strip, irresistibly drawn towards the Post Office corner. The visits became more frequent and conducted with greater urgency on each occasion. Then, as if it were meant to be, he turned up at the tennis club on the adjacent court. She found herself running around faster than ever and laughing and talking much more than usual. Although she tried as hard as she could to play well, she in fact played atrociously. She later found herself thinking about him, unable to remove him from her mind. And each night after that was the same. In the moments before sleep, in the secure bedroom darkness and in her marital bed, she fantasised about him. She imagined ways in which his exploring hands would begin the love rituals. Each following morning from these pre-sleep fantasies, she awoke to real desire.

Ilma was not a shallow person, but in anyone's lifespan a time may come when delusion intrudes, and for Ilma, her time had arrived.

Her desire deluded her into thinking a secret affair with a stranger would not destroy the values she appreciated in her marriage, or affect the lifestyle it generated. She believed she could conduct an affair without being any less dutiful as a wife. She could pursue her normal activities and retain her everyday friendships. Nobody needed to know, she thought. So where was the harm?

Oh, yes. There was the matter of loyalty, but her delusion took care of such things. It provided her with thoughts that made the whole proposition appear to be beneficial to all concerned. After all, she reasoned, a happy wife must be a better wife.

★

Her affair began in Possum Park, a recreation area to the township's north, situated on the far side of a shallow river and accessible only via an old wooden trestle bridge.

A number of caravans stood in a well-lit area of the park. Close to them were several electric barbecues with adjacent benches and tables. A cinder driving track led from the bridge to the caravan area, and beyond to the tennis club and the football oval.

On a warm Saturday evening in 1997, a small group

gathered around a barbecue bench. They were all dressed in tennis attire, having spent the afternoon playing on the nearby courts.

Amongst the group was Rod Skapleson. He managed to look elegant – even though his tennis shorts had a large red gravel stain down one side. Although not quite of average height, his slim build gave an impression of tallness. Light from a nearby lamppost shone on his clean-shaven face and brought a glitter to his smooth dark hair.

He had just joined the others who were already seated and starting to eat.

Rod, the centrepiece of Ilma's fantasies, was a recent appointee as sub-editor and only reporter for the Sandhaven and District Journal.

The Journal's owner and editor was Joseph Bernaldo. His father founded it in 1936 and Joseph acquired it upon his father's death in 1956. Joseph was then seventy and preparing for his retirement. Having no family, he named as his sole beneficiary, who so ever was the Journal's editor at the time of his death.

Joseph liked Rod. He intended to train him to become the Journal editor and business manager. He did not yet intend to tell Rod about the will.

When interviewed for the reporter job, Rod had made it clear he would have to look around for accommodation, and would require living expenses while he did this. Joseph had offered to subsidise the cost of a room at the local hotel, but they both understood this arrangement could not go on indefinitely. So when Long John Martin, a local retired fencing contractor, came into the office to place an advertisement for the sale of his old caravan at a give-away price, it gave Joseph an idea. He showed the advert to Rod and offered to lend him the money to buy the caravan. The caravan was on a leased site at Possum Park.

Two weeks before the barbecue Rod joined the Sandhaven Tennis Club. In skill he was no better than the average club player, but enjoyed the exercise and the satisfaction of occasionally hitting a good shot.

In his spare time, Rod read adventure novels – through which he obtained a superficial view of life. In most of these novels, the heroes led a fast life without working and miraculously obtained material things without effort. They got away with little white lies and drove their cars at excessive speeds – and they bedded women at the drop of a hat.

Rod had no wish to hurt anyone – but Rod was a romantic who saw himself as a hero. Through reading a lot of cheap detective stories he was conditioned to believe this kind of behaviour to be of no harm. He was an intelligent but immature man. He couldn't face up to contentious issues or intimate matters, and he kept his past to himself.

Ilma Matthews, Jan and Brian Clements, and Sally Tully were also at the barbeque. They were all close friends in their mid thirties. Ilma's husband, Vincent, a big man ten years her elder, was also present.

Sally, bright and energetic, had taken on the mantle of ensuring Rod felt welcomed within the group.

Jan and Brian were happily married – a rare example of soul mates who freely shared their thoughts and feelings. In terms of observing the comings and goings in Sandhaven Creek, they easily proved to be true to the old adage 'two pairs of eyes are better than one'.

Ilma's husband, Vincent, was tall and strong, and couldn't be pushed around easily. He was a prominent citizen, Local Citizen's Social Club President, and Headmaster at the larger of the two Sandhaven Creek primary schools. He was dedicated to the advancement and wellbeing of the township – a dedication which perhaps blinded him to the otherwise obvious restlessness of his wife.

Almost everyone in Sandhaven Creek knew of and respected Vincent Mathews. He had proved himself to be trustworthy, reliable and generous. Several town bullies had attempted to rile him, but none had succeeded in bettering him. He was, at forty-five years of age, a very confident man.

★

With most food eaten and considerable wine consumed, conversation amongst the barbecue group was in a healthy state.

There had been much talk about the chances of getting a government grant to build a communal swimming pool, and all except Rod had participated in the discussion. Realising Rod was out of touch with the topic, Sally decided to change the subject. Awaiting a lull in the conversation she raised the matter of Australia's treatment of refugees. But the issue failed to attract Rod's attention and both Vincent and Ilma become disinterested. Only Sally, Brian and Jan carried on talking about the refugee situation.

Vincent got up and walked over to the barbecue. Rod looked towards Ilma, and for the first time, he recognised her as being sexually attractive.

He remembered it was Ilma who suggested having a barbecue near the river. He had been looking at the club notice board before sitting down to afternoon tea and had overheard Ilma talking to Jan and Brian. She proposed they go straight from tennis to buy some food and drink and then meet up in the park. Vincent was away in the toilet at the time, but he supported the idea when he heard of it.

Now, while looking towards her, Rod caught what seemed to be a questioning look in Ilma's eyes as she returned his gaze. Maybe she set up this barbecue knowing he would be drawn into it, he thought. Maybe she had selected Possum Park because he was living nearby. Of course, he was flattered.

Brian Clements was facing Ilma. He also noticed the look in her eyes, but only fleetingly, and almost dismissively. He made no connection between what he saw and the barbecue being Ilma's idea. Had he done so, he would have been worried. Brian was protective of Ilma, who he had known since she and Jan were his classmates in primary school. Although only months separated all three, Ilma was the youngest and had always been the smallest.

Brian was happy that Ilma had married Vincent, who she started dating just after leaving high school. Despite the age gap, Vincent and Brian had been good friends for many years ever since. At the age of eighteen, Brian had first beaten Vincent in a tennis match, and afterwards Vincent had bought him his first pub drink.

Brian had met Rod a couple of times. Although he found him easy to get on with, Brian was naturally cautious with strangers. He and Jan had both noticed Rod didn't give much away about himself, so suspicion in regard to the nature of Ilma's eye contact should have come easily. However, a question from Sally kept Brian's concentration on the refugee conversation, and the possible warning of a pending indiscretion was lost forever.

Rod had now got the message and it excited him, but being naturally cagey, he didn't respond directly. He instead reached for a half full bottle of red wine and turned his attention to Vincent.

Rod already knew something of Vincent's character and interests. He had told Joe Bernaldo about joining the tennis club, and Joe, who approved of Rod getting involved in community activities, acquainted Rod with the background of some club members. He was particularly informative about Vincent and Brian, even going so far as to apprise Rod of their hobbies.

Mindful of this information, Rod started up a conversation with Vincent.

"Have some more wine," he offered, smiling disarmingly, while holding the bottle over Vincent's less than half empty glass.

Vincent, whose mind had been wandering, was a bit startled. "Oh, yes, right," he answered, lifting his glass. "It's a good drop," he observed politely. "What is it?"

"Lehman's, Clancy Red. Not too expensive really. I bought it in the pub bottle shop – to celebrate my new home." Rod's normally low-pitched voice was deliberately raised to draw attention.

"How are you settling in?" Vincent enquired as he brushed a fly off the rim of his glass.

"No problems really," replied Rod. "Living in a caravan is quite good actually, not much housework to be done." He paused, "More time for other things," he added, wondering if Ilma had yet picked up on the conversation, but kept his face turned towards Vincent.

Vincent, still having trouble with the fly, didn't see the slightly mocking look in Rod's brown eyes. Keen to be friendly to a new community member, he carried on chatting. "Is the van in good condition?"

"Not bad really," answered Rod, inwardly pleased to receive a question from which he could manufacture a useful bait. "The caravan is quite comfortable, but needs a bit of paint on the outside," he added. "Oh yes, and the door is hard to close."

Vincent took the bait. "What is wrong with the door?"

"It needs the hinges replacing," Rod replied, returning his voice to its normal level.

"It doesn't sound much of a problem," said Vincent. "Are they screw fixed, or welded?"

"I don't know. Haven't given it much thought. Not much of a handyman, you know. I am more into books."

"Well, you know, I'm a bit the opposite. I don't read much these days but I like woodwork, I like the feel of dressed wood. I've quite a good little workshop at home."

The others at the table had gone quiet. Vincent paused and glanced around before picking up the bottle. "What about you, Jan? Your glass is empty. And yours too, Ilma," he said, topping up their glasses. "We're talking about Rod's new acquisition. You know, he told us about it when he turned up at tennis. He bought Long John Martin's old blue caravan," he said pointing to a caravan near the end of a row behind them.

Rod glanced at Ilma's face. She has caught on, he thought. He felt pleased with himself for Ilma now knew which caravan was his.

And then, as if on cue, Ilma raised her newly filled glass, smiled across the table at Rod and said, "Cheers everyone, let's toast Rod's new home. Here's to the caravan." She paused, then continued. "And here's to the Gypsy who lives in it. Welcome to Sandhaven Creek, Rod."

"Yes," said Vincent. "Welcome to Sandhaven Creek, and now you're a resident, how about joining our local social club. The facilities are excellent and include a couple of snooker tables, and a gaming room. Oh, and we run a darts club on Thursday evenings if you're interested and there is bridge on Tuesdays and bingo on Friday nights. The cafeteria is open every evening except Sunday. The meals are cheap. You can get three courses and a glass of house red for twelve dollars." Vincent paused, looked at Brian, and then turned his attention back to Rod. "I'll nominate you if you like, Rod," he said. "Brian can second it."

Dismissing any reservations, Brian agreed. "You can come as my guest and try it out. How about Saturday night, we could eat there?"

"Well I'd sure like to, and I did intend to apply for membership. My Boss, Joe Bernaldo mentioned a club I should join, and I expect it's the same one. However, I'm not sure about next Saturday; it may have to be Saturday week. Can I ring you after I've checked out my work situation?"

"Yes. We usually go anyway, so it will be fine."

Ilma, well aware the caravan discussion between Rod and Vincent could be used to her advantage, was awaiting her chance. She had been covertly watching Rod and was now sure of her ground. The caravan could become the medium through which she could open the door to a closer relationship with Rod. The thought excited her, but with the instinct of a hunter, she kept her cool and patiently awaited an opportunity to strike.

Her moment came when there was a break in the general conversation around the table. Quickly, and before anyone else could interrupt, she turned toward Rod and asked, "I heard you say something to Vince about a door problem. What was it all about?"

"The caravan door hinges are broken," replied Rod, with an inwardly thankful sigh. "But I'm not into carpentry. My tool kit only consists of a hammer, a screwdriver and a pair of pliers. And I have lost the screwdriver anyway."

Ilma chipped in, "Ooo, you aren't like Vincent. Vince has more tools than a hardware shop. Always making, something. Maybe he can help you. What about it, Vince?" she said gaily, as if helping Rod will be good fun for Vincent.

Vincent, however, was not pleased at the question, but refusing to help to anyone was not in his nature and he didn't want to make Ilma look silly.

"Happy to try, Rod, perhaps we can go and have a look at it."

"Sure. You mean now?"

"Why not?"

As Rod and Vincent got up from the table, Ilma rose to her feet at the same time. "Excuse us," she said to the others, taking hold of Vincent's hand in a slow possessive sort of way for everyone to see. The three walked towards the caravan.

Jan looked at Sally. "Gosh," she whispered. "She can talk him into anything."

"Yes," agreed Brian. "Vince is a bit of a goose, but I'm certain Ilma doesn't wear the pants for the big issues. Vincent is absolutely devoted to her but he isn't stupid, he can put his foot down when he wants to."

Keen to keep the conversation from returning to the refugee subject, Brian turned to Sally and asked, "What about you Sally? Is there anything going on between you, and Rod?"

Sally shrugged. "No," she replied with a laugh. "I partnered him on his first day at the tennis club and we went for a drink together afterwards. We're just friends, nothing else." Sally paused and smiled. "Do you know," she continued. "He's only twenty-six, and anyway he's not tall enough for me, I prefer someone my own size."

"He has a swarthy complexion, I wonder if he has Spanish ancestors?"

Sally smiled, "I've already asked him," she declared. "He claims to be a third generation Australian of English descent."

"Still," said Jan. "He's quite good looking in a dark sinister sort of way. Not the fair Nordic type, like you, dear." She gave Brian a bit of a hug.

★

Ilma gazed around at the caravan interior. It had an open-plan arrangement in matching blue décor of light and dark shades, and contained all the usual things plus a bookcase, a television, a video recorder, a stereo system and a microwave oven.

Standing close to the bookcase, she looked at the titles on the top shelf.

"I see, Rod, you like reading Beryl Bainbridge," she said, fingering a leather marker protruding from a small paperback book. "I liked her first novel best, 'The Dressmaker'. They made a movie from it. Golly, it was such a terrific black comedy, it had me shivering at times. Actually, I bought the book after seeing the film. Have you read 'The Dressmaker', Rod?"

Rod saw Ilma in a new light. "Yes. I have read it, quite a thriller. Didn't see the movie, it was a bit before my time. I've read most of her novels. They are not the sort of stories I normally read, but somebody gave me one of her books, and I found I liked it. In her latest novel, 'Every Man For Himself', I have to agree with the critics, she captures the era very well. It's a very good read from start to finish." He got up and stood beside the table.

Vincent rose from his seat, book talk was not for him. "Let's see if the existing hinges will come off easily," he said, walking towards the door. "I have a large screwdriver in the car. Won't be long." He called out as he left the caravan and headed towards the car park.

Ilma crouched low to examine the books on the lower

shelves. Her short white tennis skirt fell back to expose her thighs, and from his elevated position standing beside the table, Rod could see down the cleavage between her breasts. He was surprised he had not noticed her body earlier. Her skin was so smooth, even though she was very suntanned. But then, it was not her body that had first attracted him to her. Nor was it the shape of her face, for it was not classically beautiful, and it was not her bottle-blonde hair either, because it could have been any colour in its natural state. No, it was something else, something to do with her smile and the sensuality of her lips, and the challenging look in her eyes which called for a response.

"Do we go on talking about books?" Ilma said, looking up at him. "I mean we could be talking about you. You look intelligent, what brings you to a small country town like this? An ex-girlfriend? Or did you rob a bank in the big smoke? Or shouldn't I ask?"

Rod grinned. "Well, there is an ex-girlfriend, about three years ex actually. But I didn't rob a bank. No, I just came here to get some job experience for a while, although Joe Bernaldo has made me an attractive offer to make me stay on permanently. I am thinking about it, but haven't really decided yet."

Ilma got up and stood beside him. "And has anything happened which may make your stay more interesting," she says, looking him straight in the eye, her face slowly breaking into a smile.

"Maybe," he said. "I'm still trying to decide. I think when you suggested the barbecue you knew Jan would include Sally, and you guessed Sally would bring me. Didn't you?"

"Yes. It seemed likely." Ilma paused, and her expression became more serious. "You're not offended are you?"

"Well now, I guess it depends on why you wanted me to come." Rod replied, his eyes widening in an innocent expression.

"I think you know the answer already, Rod." Ilma smiled.

"Suppose you tell me though, just for me to be sure." Rod said, encouragingly.

Ilma moved closer to him. Stretching out an arm, she brushed a speck of dirt off his shirt collar. "God," she said. "You don't believe in making things easy, do you? You're a mysterious stranger, and I'm bored and inquisitive. So can we begin there?"

Rod, well aware of her closeness, was still cautious. He remained motionless. Without expression, he said, "So why are you bored? I mean, you seemed to be happy enough at tennis, and I bet you don't want for much."

Ilma left his collar alone and rested her hand on his shoulder, "Ah, if only you knew. This is a small town, Rod. I meet and talk to the same people week after week. It's not a place full of fun, and Vince is all wrapped up in community service and everyone expects me to lead an absolutely respectable life."

"And you don't want a respectable life?"

Ilma took time to think about her answer. She felt her heart beat faster, knowing she was about to make a committal. "No, it's not really me," she said. She paused, realising she had revealed the truth to herself. "In loyalty to Vince I try to be conventional, but it's quite an effort," she sighed. "I'm more of a free spirit than is expected in this town, and if I wasn't married to Vince, I'd be living in a big exciting city with plenty of night life."

"And, Vincent? How do you feel about him?"

Ilma's light touch on his shoulder became heavier. "Well, let me tell you quite honestly, Rod. I think Vince is a dear, and I know he's a devoted husband, and I want to continue to be his wife, but although he's very generous and lets me twist him around my little finger, romantically he can be very dull.

There was a moment of silence. Her jaw line stiffened as she looked directly into Rod's eyes, "I certainly don't want to hurt Vince, but the fact is I need more stimulation than he can give."

"And when did you decide I might offer whatever it is you are missing?"

Ilma relaxed and playfully walked her fingers from his shoulder, down his shirt and across his chest. She giggled. "Oh, about two weeks ago when you joined the tennis club. You were talking to Sally and arranging to go for a meal with her. I could tell there was nothing serious between you, and I thought to myself, what a waste, who's going to pick him up? He is young, good looking, and obviously educated. I doubt if more than a dozen men in the whole of this town fits a similar description."

Rod's face was expressionless. He looked at her for a while. "So it's just a bit of a fling you're looking for? Pretty dangerous stuff, if as you say everybody in the town knows you. Vince would soon hear about it."

Ilma stepped even closer to him. She lowered her voice.

"Oh, don't get me wrong, I'm not interested in just a one night stand, I want something more intimate. I need a bit of inner self-sharing with someone for a while. And Vince is not going to get to know, because —"

Rod interrupted her. "He will, if you keep talking like this. He's coming back along the path," he said, quickly drawing back half a pace.

Ilma touched Rod's shoulder once more, this time running her fingers down his bare arm. He could feel the electricity in the contact. "Will I see you again soon?" she asked.

"Could be," Rod replied, hastily re-seating himself at the table as Vincent reached the door.

Grinning as he entered the caravan, Vincent placed a small yellow-handled screwdriver down on the table. "I found this in the grass, just a couple of metres from your door. Now your hammer and pliers won't feel so lonely."

Rod picked it up and examined it, thankful he didn't have to look Vincent in the eye straight away. "Yes, it's mine," he said, pushing it around.

Vince had also brought a much larger screwdriver. He began to loosen the door hinge screws. "They will come out, no problem," he said. "If it's convenient I'll come over in the morning and swap the hinges over for you. I'll leave this here," he said, placing the large screwdriver alongside the smaller one. He sat down beside Ilma who had sidled into the corner seat across the table from Rod.

As they spoke, Rod could see Ilma was in danger of becoming too effusive. He felt uncomfortable being so close to her in Vincent's company. He was relieved when

Vincent finally looked at his watch and said, "Best we go and help clean up from the barbecue. It's nearly ten thirty." He opened the door for Ilma, let her go first and then followed her out.

"I'll follow you in a couple of minutes, something I have to do." Rod said. He waited until they were half way along the path before he quietly closed the door and turned towards the bed.

Under the bed were two long and deep drawers, one beside the other. He pulled out the right hand one to reveal a very comprehensive set of carpentry tools, including an electric drill and a sander.

"Better not let you see these, Vince," he whispered to himself as he threw his own small screwdriver in amongst them and quickly closed the drawer.

2
The Call

Making news, Saturday 15 February 1997:
Representatives of over sixty countries have agreed to open up their telecommunications markets. The decision is likely to generate more rapid technological advancement in the telly industry – particularly for those living in remote Australian townships.

Comment:
This news item may have caught the eye of a particular Sandhaven Creek resident – for whom a personal mobile phone would have been an advantage at the time.

On the way home in the car, Ilma sat rather quietly, trying to keep an emotional cauldron under control. Mixed feelings of guilt, fear, sorrow and excitement caused her heart to flutter. She could hardly believe what she had done.

For the past week she had been thinking about Rod and the possibility of them having an affair. The thoughts had been dreamlike figments of her imagination which were devoid of any responsibility. Then, impulsively, and without any awareness of possible consequences, she had decided to turn her dreams into reality. It had all seemed so easy at the time.

Indeed so it had been, but then, in those few minutes alone in the caravan with Rod, she had exposed her soul. She understood her future was now in his hands, and as a result, her relationship to Vince may be changed forever. She knew a favourable response from Rod could bring her the excitement she craved but feared an unfavourable response reaching Vincent's ears. To preserve her marriage and to protect Vincent's reputation, she needed to keep what had just happened, and whatever may happen, as secret as possible.

Somewhere inside her, a little warning bell rang. It dawned on her that she had started something which was already out of control. If Rod responded to her advances, she could hardly now tell him it was all a mistake, nothing more than a harmless bit of fun, just a little flirting. Imagine how Rod would feel, she thought. Nobody wants to be made a fool of and he could easily decide to put it around she was a loose woman. This would soon reach Vincent's ears.

On the other hand, if she did take Rod as a lover, and Vincent found out, she could be putting Rod in terrible danger. She had never seen Vincent lose his cool, but every man has his limit. Yet she knew she found Rod too alluring to resist, given half the chance.

She sat beside her husband, driving home with him as they had done together so many times before. But this time with a tension between them – a tension which only she was aware of.

Ilma slumped back into the corner of her seat so that Vincent couldn't see her face unless taking his eyes off the road. She looked at Vincent, appreciating his size and strength. She had always felt safe in his care. Behind his air of confidence, which was always on display, she wondered if Vincent was really happy. What if in fact he did not like being the dependable citizen with a predictable future? Perhaps, she thought, he too had secret desires to be free of responsibility, to see new things, explore new relationships, and generally live life to the full.

Ilma couldn't recall if she and Vince had ever discussed such matters. In all their years of marriage they have never talked about themselves, never asked each other the questions which would reveal their inner thoughts. She had never attempted to push the boundaries of truth, in case it hurt their relationship. Perhaps she had been wrong in this. Perhaps she had been too content to see Vince only from the outside and this had limited the intimacy between them.

These thoughts saddened her. She wanted to reach out and touch Vince. No, not at this moment. Not now. Not while she was awaiting Rod's answer to her invitation to commence an illicit affair. And not while she inwardly wished for the answer to be yes.

To Ilma, her intended affair with Rod was like the product of an awakening dream, still unreal but somewhat confused with actual events. Rod hovered around in her mind, but life with Vincent went on.

★

When they arrived home, Vince went into the kitchen and put on the kettle. Ilma followed him but stayed only long enough to say she felt a bit fuzzy after all the red wine and was going straight to bed. Vince nodded. "Okay love," he said before giving her a light kiss on her cheek.

He made himself a cup of coffee and carried it into the living room, switched on the T.V. and sat down to await the late news review. He found himself watching the last few minutes of a sextravaganza of almost pornographic standard, and he was amazed at the antics of a near naked couple attempting to make love in a rowing boat. He recognised the scene as a fantasy and it did not sexually arouse him. His life with Ilma was sufficiently satisfying, even though sex between them was less frequent than it used to be.

The film finished and the adverts started. An ad for a video camera, which Vincent was planning to buy Ilma as a birthday gift, appeared on the T.V. screen. Ironically, he recalled she had only given him a tennis hat for his birthday. Oh well, he thought. She does have many other qualities.

He turned his thoughts to Rod. He wondered what his background was and whether he would settle in to a country town life. Not many young people stayed in the town for very long. It isn't a young person's scene. And this, of course, was why it was so important to make young people like Rod welcome, for without them the town would surely die.

Vincent hoped Rod would prove worthy of the attention he was getting, but somewhere in Vincent's mind there was a little niggling doubt.

★

Making news, Sunday 16 February 1997:
The Laurence Olivier Theatre Awards for the past season were announced in London today. Award for Best New Play goes to 'Stanley'.

Comment:
Sandhaven Creek had an amateur theatrical society. It operated out of an old cheese factory building and produced four shows each year. Two years ago, Ilma Mathews had a small supporting role in a summer production. She played the part of a schoolgirl.

In the garden on a Sunday afternoon, Ilma and Vincent were cutting back the branches of a tree which were too close to the rotary clothes hoist. Ilma, who was very agile, had commandeered the ladder and was attacking the higher branches with heavy-duty pruning clippers. Vincent was sawing through the thicker lower limbs.

Ilma was pleased to have something to do which required both physical and mental effort. It prevented her from thinking too much about Rod, and from worrying about Vincent. Helping out Vincent with this particular gardening task somehow made her feel less guilty about her deceitful intentions. She had always enjoyed working with Vincent on house and garden projects. They worked well as a team. She was quick, nimble and artistic, while Vincent was strong, handy and technically knowledgeable.

Vincent too was pleased. With Ilma alongside him he

felt energised and hard work seemed much easier to carry out. It was always like this when they worked together. He found the time passed quickly, but within its span there was usually a moment which seems to last forever. He paused for a rest. He watched Ilma stretching up on tiptoes and leaning over the ladder top, knee-length jeans taut around her trim bottom, yellow halter top displaying her bare brown shoulders, arms reaching out as far as they will go, and hair all tousled from brushing through the tree branches. Looking, he thought, like a twenty year old girl. Immediately he experienced a sudden intense feeling of both love and pride.

It was unfortunate that Vincent was not the kind of man who could easily vocalise his feelings, for had he done so then, it was quite probable Ilma would have abandoned her deceitful plan.

★

Making news, Monday 17 February 1997:
Former high-school teacher Christophe Augin has set a new world record for a solo 'round the world sail'. She completed the journey in 105 days, 20 hours and 31 minutes.

Comment:
It was a full day's drive from Sandhaven Creek to the nearest shoreline. Sailing therefore was not an option for teachers at Vincent's school, but some of them did enjoy canoeing on the local river.

On Monday morning at about ten o'clock, Ilma heard the phone ring and picked up the receiver. "Ilma Mathews speaking," she said.

There was a pause, then she heard Rod's voice, "Hello, Ilma."

Ilma had spent the weekend wondering what to do should Rod contact her. The doubts and recriminations had fought against her lustful desire to be with Rod. She had told herself over and over again she must not go through with this. She would try to tell Rod in such a way as to maintain his friendship and trust. She had even considered telling Vincent what she had done, and how wrong she knew it was. But the sound of Rod's voice seduced her immediately, and she instantly knew the direction to go.

She found herself trembling as she responded, "Oh Rod, it's you."

"Are you alone?"

"Yes."

"I thought we should continue where we left off."

There was no need for Ilma to wonder any more. Her reaction to Rod's suggestion was nature driven and her reply was given without thought of guilt or consequence. "Ooo, what a good idea," she said, fiddling with a pencil on the phone table and trying hard to sound at ease.

"You were about to tell me why Vincent won't find out about any little clandestine meetings we may have. How can you be so sure?"

"Mmm, clandestine meetings sound exciting," Ilma responded with amusement. "It conjures up all sorts of mischief. But to ally your fears, well, we won't meet each other in Sandhaven Creek except, of course, on social occasions."

Rod was puzzled but he pressed on. With a trace of irritation in his voice he asked, "So where will we meet? Not somewhere out in the bush I hope?"

"No, pet. Somewhere, more comfortable. Either in Dareboolah, or in Tamworth."

"And where on earth is Dareboolah?"

"It's a small township just this side of Tamworth, less than an hour's drive."

"Are you kidding, why there?"

Ilma felt she has created an air of mystery and could now control the conversation. She stopped pushing the pencil around and became more relaxed. Her voice firmed up as she replied, "Because I own an art gallery in Dareboolah."

"I didn't know you to be a working girl, I thought your time was your own," Rod said, sounding surprised.

"I'm not really," Ilma said. "Well not at the gallery, anyway. I have someone who manages the business for me, but I like to meet any new artists personally and give my approval to all new artworks. I attend the gallery every Thursday to do this. A lot of my artists have day jobs in Tamworth and I often have to see them in the evening. There's a small studio apartment attached to the gallery and most times I stay there overnight. It enables me to shop in Tamworth the next morning."

"And Vincent? What about Vincent. What is his interest in the gallery?"

"Oh, he doesn't ever come. It's not his scene and he is

quite happy about the arrangement because he plays in a darts team in a Thursday night competition, and he is never home much before midnight. To keep our relationship on an even keel I make a point of being first home on Fridays, so we can have a drink together before dinner."

There was silence for a moment. Ilma was afraid she may not have convinced Rod they could safely meet in Dareboolah or Tamworth. But Rod was only being thoughtful.

"I see," he said. "And I suppose you just happen to know I have to be in Tamworth every Thursday, to pick up the Journal advertising copy, and cover the evening Harness Race meetings?"

Rod was hooked and Ilma could sense it. "Of course Rod," she replied. "And rest assured Vincent knows this too because your predecessor, Tom Burden, a rather fat and pimply youth with ridiculously long hair also covered the Harness Races. He used to give Vincent tips to pass on to his darts team mates." Ilma paused to add effect, "So you can see," she continued, "Vince won't be surprised if you and I are occasionally seen in Tamworth on the same day. Will he?"

"I suppose you're right. But look, I have to go. The boss is coming this way. Have you got a gallery card?"

"Yes, of course."

"Well, in case I can't get to tennis, I'll accept Brian's offer to take me to the social club for dinner next Saturday week. See if you and Vince can join us, and bring me a card."

Ilma was delighted. In her excitement she could hardly

keep her voice under control. She was going to have an affair with this ravishingly sexy man. She, Ilma, the girl who had been leading the life of a country town housewife, was about to break out of its repressive hold. About to savour the sexual freedom she was unconsciously been missing. About to explore her sensuality, as she had always wanted to, and may have been able to do, had she remained single and lived in a big city. Delighted and excited as she was though, she was also a little frightened.

"Rod."

"Yes."

"I'm glad you called. But please don't phone me at home again. What if Vincent had answered?"

Rod laughed, "Oh I had the perfect excuse ready," he said, "I would have thanked him for fixing my door. See you Saturday, or a week on Saturday."

"Rod, I…" Ilma stopped speaking, for Rod had hung up.

★

Ten minutes later, the phone rang again. Ilma heard it as she walked back from the mailbox at the garden gate. She hurried into the house to answer it. Breathlessly and with excited anticipation, she picked up the receiver. "Ilma Mathews speaking." She gushed.

"Yes love, I know. You sound out of breath. Been on the exercise bike?"

"Oh. No, Vince. I've been getting the mail. I rushed back in when I heard the phone. I was expecting a call from Nardia."

"Is there anything in the mail worth mentioning?"

"There are three envelopes. I haven't opened any yet but none look interesting, unless you've developed a morbid attraction to bills."

"Not really. Look I'm ringing from Olsen's Bookshop. I left a book on the lounge coffee table and I need to know the title and the author's name. I have to order some copies for the school."

"Hang on, I'll go and get it."

Ilma was glad she had been a little out of breath when picking up the phone, for on hearing Vincent's voice she felt herself trembling, and would have found it hard to keep her voice normal. Suddenly she was acutely aware she was playing a dangerous game, and how hard it would be to control her feelings in Vincent's presence.

In the week's remaining days, Ilma tried her best to remain outwardly calm, although she was inwardly excited at the thought of seeing Rod on Saturday. But Rod did not attend tennis on the Saturday, and in the tea break Ilma learnt from Jan that he had gone to Tamworth for the day to cover some sports carnival, and had asked Brian if the Social Club dinner meeting can be put back to the following Saturday.

Disappointments did not come easily to Ilma. In consequence, Vincent suffered some minor irritations — particularly in the timing and quality of their meals over the following week. But Ilma put him off the scent by telling him she had problems with her part-time work at the library and was sorry if she seemed a bit edgy.

3
Party Plans

Making news, Tuesday 18 February 1997:
Over three hundred people are missing and thought to be killed following a mud slide in Peru. The slide has destroyed two villages in hilly country southwest of Lima. The terrain is making it difficult for rescuers to reach the victims.

Comment:
The landscape surrounding Sandhaven Creek was relatively flat, but during the town's oldest residents lifetime, the river had never flooded. The locality was not earthquake prone and no one living in the district had ever seen a whirlwind. Natural disasters just did not happen in Sandhaven Creek and nobody thought of such things. Least of all Vincent Mathews, who had other things on his mind today...

On Tuesday morning, Vincent decided to go to the camera shop and buy Ilma's present. Ilma had taken some photos recently, at a local charity function in which Vincent had officiated, and he knew she was anxious to have them developed. If he volunteered to take them, he thought, it would disguise the fact he was going to the shop to buy a camera.

He went into the kitchen to find Ilma washing her

breakfast dishes, dressed in her tennis gear. Vincent thought she looked very sexy standing there, legs firmly placed and hands rapidly moving over the sink. He wanted to put his arms around her and kiss the back of her neck, but he understood she is was in a hurry to get to tennis, and he let the moment slip away. He checked the contents of his wallet, took his keys off the key rack, and said, "I have to make a couple of calls in the main street today. If you'll give me your camera, I'll take the film out and get it developed."

Ilma's face was set. She was in a sour mood. She had been thinking, on the pretence of their news value, she may have used the pictures as an excuse to see Rod. But then she knew Vincent would not like the idea of them being published, and to suggest such a thing would only bring about a fight with him. He was so hide bound about respectability. She recognised there were certain things she would be unable to persuade him to agree with, even if she used her considerable feminine charms.

She nodded towards the kitchen bench end. "It's over there," she said, rather sharply. "And can you get some milk, we have none left in the fridge and I'm not going to have time to stop."

Vince couldn't quite get the logic of this, since she would have plenty of time on the way home. He felt slightly challenged but didn't know why. "Okay, see you later." He picked up the camera, extracted the film, and set out on his shopping trip.

Vincent put in many extra hours at school in the evenings, yet seldom took time off while classes were in session. This morning, however, was an exception, for he had advised his senior staff yesterday not to expect him at school before eleven thirty.

He had given himself plenty of time to do what he had to do, so he decided to put his car in the Town Hall car park and take a leisurely walk along Main Street.

The sun was out and the air felt clean and healthy. There were several who nodded or waved to him, for Main Street was already busy with shoppers and others going about their business, and many people recognised him. The mix of cars in the street included a number of farm trucks and utilities, and most men he could see were wearing jeans and check shirts. The shop buildings were either single or double storey, with only the Town Hall standing higher. The main street, which is Main Street, was four cars wide, with generous pavements on each side, all lined with parking meters. The meters remained inactive unless a stranger visited the town, for everyone knew the Council did not employ a parking inspector.

There was great variety to the shop fronts, a few were built of timber and dated back to the mid nineteenth century, with some in original form, some remodelled, and some new. The more recent buildings had been constructed in brick. And almost all the shops, new and old, had a canopy extending over the footpath, so there was little space for trees except in the City Square and in Town Hall Square. To make up for the lack of natural greenery along the pavement line, the Council had provided a number of planter boxes.

Vincent liked the township appearance and considered

it to be of true Australian outback character.

In the mornings, Sandhaven Creek was a bustling place, but the afternoons brought the heat and humidity, which drove most people into somewhere naturally shady or into air-conditioned premises.

Vincent enjoyed his walk. It was his town, everything in it was familiar to him. He knew the town had seen some hard times, and he was proud to have played a part in its survival.

He entered the photography section of an electrical goods shop and asked for Alex Chapman, the Store Manager.

Alex was probably the only shopkeeper in Sandhaven Creek who wore a suit. The one he had on doesn't really fit him, particularly around his ample waist. He flashed a smile which revealed a gold tooth.

"G'day Vince, Mate," he said. "What can I do for ya? Still interested in the camera?"

"Yes, Alex. The S.L.R. 160 digital video you showed me last week. Do you still have one in stock?"

"Sure, Mate. Ya wanna see it again? No trouble."

"No. it's alright. I had a good look at it already. What is your price on it? I mean your bottom price, Alex."

"It's marked at $2,090. But give us a minute and I might be able to knock a bit off for ya."

Vincent stared at him, having played this game before. "I hope so, Alex," he said, "because I can buy it at the camera shop for less."

"Well, seein' as how yer the club President, suppose I gives yer a special price. Let's see, say ten percent off. 'Ow does that sound?"

"Ten percent off the camera shop price, or ten percent off your price?"

"Oh, okay. For ya. $1,800, cash. Fair enough, mate?"

Vincent laughed, "Fair enough, Alex. How do you want me to pay for it?"

"Ya can give me a cheque if ya want."

"No, I'd rather put it on my credit card. It's a present for Ilma, and if I write a cheque out for such a large sum Ilma will want to know what I've been buying. And please, Alex, this is top secret, don't mention it at the club or Ilma will get to know."

"I wouldn't dare, Mate. I suppose ya want it gift wrapped. 'Ow is ya lovely wife then? Keeping ya happy, is she?"

Alex went off to a storeroom and came back with a box. He made a good job of wrapping it, and then put it into a plastic shop bag and handed it over. "It's all in here, mate," he said. "Complete with carry case, instruction book, and warranty. Tell ya missus ta be careful opening the box, there's a lot of those bloody packing bubbles in it."

Vincent handed over Ilma's roll of film and ordered some prints. They exchanged a few pleasantries and Vincent left the shop carrying the bag. He walked along Main Street until he came to Brian Clement's office. Through the office window he could see Brian at his desk, and alone. He tapped on the window and Brian reacted with a smile and motioned for him to come in. Vincent entered Brian's reception room and nodded to Brian's Secretary, Maureen O'Donavan, an ex-pupil of Vincent's school.

"Good morning Maureen, how are things with you on this lovely sunny day?" He greeted her.

"Oh. Hello, Mr. Mathews. I'm surprised to see you here at this hour. Is Brian expecting you?"

Vincent grinned. "He is now. We just communicated through the window. I think he's a bit surprised too, but he waved for me to go on in. Has he got any appointments lined up? I want a bit of time with him."

"He has no appointments until this afternoon. Would you like a coffee? Milk and one sugar, isn't it?"

"Yes, thanks Maureen." Vincent went over to Brian's door, politely knocked and momentarily paused, then entered without waiting for any acknowledgement. Brian motioned him to a chair.

"This isn't your usual calling time, Vince."

"My Deputy, Irene Hendry, is holding the fort for me for a couple of hours. Come to think of it, it must be five years since I last took time out."

"Yes Vince, I know. Everyone calls you the Principled Principal. Would you like a coffee?"

"Thanks. Maureen is already making me one, although I have only dropped in to thank you for lending your home for Ilma's surprise party, and to go through a few details with you." Vincent paused and held up the bag. "Oh, and this is Ilma's present. I want to give it to her at the party, and I thought you might take it home and keep it hidden for me. I'm going to give her some little thing over breakfast to put her off the scent. Talking of which, have you spoken to Rod and explained the situation of how we were using him as a decoy, pretending we would be at the club on Saturday as usual? And you did of course invite him to the party?"

"Yes. I managed to get him on the phone this morning. He seemed quite pleased at the thought of getting to know some local celebrities, and he's quite happy to wait another week to have dinner at the club. I stressed he should be careful not to mention the party if he goes to tennis on Saturday. There's one catch though, he asked if his photographer can come to take some photos. I told him you'd let him know. You don't have any objections, do you?"

"Ummm, I suppose not. Has everyone accepted the invites?"

"Yep. Jillian Parker, the librarian, Sam and Betty Isherwood, Contessa Ralstone, Florian Robbins, Sally and Rod and four from the tennis club whom Sally is inviting, and Trish and Leonard Woodhouse who Jan reckons Ilma gets on very well with at the book club meetings. I hope Florian behaves himself, Jan is not exactly over the moon at having him at the party, he is so full of himself."

"Yes. Sorry about including him but he's one of Ilma's best paying artists at the gallery, and she seems to consider him as a friend."

"What's Contessa Ralstone like? I've seen her in the street but I haven't met her."

"Oh, she's okay. She has been here now about three years or so. Ilma has had her over to dinner a few times, wants to match her up with someone, but hasn't yet succeeded. She's quite a good looking woman but too intellectual for the local lads. Good sculptor, or is it sculptress. Real images. Not broomsticks and string."

"How does Ilma know the Isherwoods?"

"Betty is a friend of Ilma's from uni days. I think they meet together for coffee sometimes, when Ilma is in Tamworth. Jillian Parker knows her very well, they worked together at the Armidale Library for several years. I understand the Isherwoods are going to stay over at Jillian's rather than drive home to Tamworth on Saturday night."

Brian was about to ask a question when Maureen entered the room with two cups of coffee on a small tray. "They both have milk and this one has the sugar," she announced, placing the tray on the desk and pointing to a cup. "I knew you would want one as well," she added, addressing Brian, who smiled at her and nodded. She stood there a little expectantly.

"We're plotting, Maureen. We're planning a surprise Saturday night birthday party. It's for Vincent's wife. You know? A surprise. No one is to know," Vincent said.

"Ooo, sounds exciting. She'll like a party. Mum's the word Mr. Mathews. I hope it's a great success," she said before leaving them to continue their plotting.

Brian was silent for a moment, trying to remember what was on his mind before Maureen interrupted them. He sipped his coffee and asked, "What about the decorations. Do you still want to do them on Friday night? How will you get out of bingo and over to my place without Ilma twigging something is up?"

"Oh, we should knock it over in an hour. Bill can look after the bingo calling, and I'll tell Ilma I have to see you for an hour or so to go over the S.C. audit report with you. What about the cake? Is it all in hand?"

"Yes. Sally is organising it. She is helping Jan with the cooking. There'll be plenty to eat, you can bet on it. Oh, and the drinks bill comes to about one hundred and fifty bucks. Pay me any time."

There was another moments silence.

"Look Vince, as your accountant I have to say this. It's only a few months since you bought Ilma a new car, and I know from her books you supplemented the gallery income last year. Don't think I'm prying, Vince, I'm just worried you may be going a bit overboard with your generosity."

"Oh, you know how it is, Brian. Ilma likes parties and I've never given her one before."

Vincent's tone became more serious as he confessed, "You know I'll do anything for Ilma. I'm ten years older than Ilma and I know in another fifteen years my working life will be over. So I give her what I can, when I can. I inherited a little money when my uncle died six years ago. It's not enough to make much difference to my retirement, so I might as well spend some of it. And what better way than to make Ilma happy."

Brian shrugged, so Vincent continued. "Well thanks for all your help. You and Jan have been fantastic. Ilma will get a kick out of it." He finished his coffee and got up.

"Well, must be off to school," he said, reaching for the door handle. "Don't forget, Friday evening we're supposed to be auditing the S.C. books."

Walking back down the street towards his car, Vincent

reflected on the comment he made to Brian about his working life being over in fifteen years. Like many other people he had suppressed the idea of retirement. Work and other responsibilities had kept him too busy to give it any serious thought. Of course, he had always wanted to see more of the world. He often imagined relaxing beside a tropical pool in the Caribbean or some similarly exotic place – with Ilma still young enough to turn heads and do justice to a bikini.

Looked at in this light, the idea of retirement did not hold any daunting prospects, but it did raise some questions, for they couldn't go on holiday forever.

As a school Principal he would get a good pension and, if he heeded Brian's warning, there would be enough of his inheritance left to do a little travelling. But would Ilma want to stay in Sandhaven Creek, when there is no further necessity to do so? They both had their roots in the town, and he would be happy to stay, but he knew Ilma was only here out of loyalty to him, and would prefer to be near the city night life.

If this was what Ilma wanted, then perhaps he should consider transferring to a city school while this was still possible, say before his fiftieth birthday, or shortly afterwards. The Education Department liked Principals to stay for at least five years after appointment, so he had better be able to offer them at least six or seven years at a new school before there was any suggestion of retirement.

He would mind if he had to leave, but he would do it for Ilma. He thought about this and he was buoyed at the thought of how, with Ilma beside him they would soon settle in and make new friends anywhere they went.

It dawned on him they must form a proper retirement plan and he should discuss the subject with Ilma.

As he approached his car he made a mental note to do so – after the birthday party was behind them.

4
The Present

Making news, Friday 21 February 1997:
Zoran Djindjic, the Serbian Democratic Party Leader, takes over as Mayor of Belgrade. He is now the most politically powerful opponent to Serbian President Slobodan Milosevic, who leads the Socialist Party.

Comment:
Alex Chapman was often referred to as the Greek, although he was actually second generation Serb. He may have been the only resident in Sandhaven Creek to take any notice of this political news item. One other resident was more interested in having a bath.

While Ilma finished washing up the dinner dishes, Vincent was on his way to Brian's house on a secret mission to decorate for the coming party. Ilma reflected it was the first time she has cooked on a Friday, since the 'Bingo in the Bistro' evenings had resumed at the club, shortly after the Christmas break. Five weeks of club food and dreary company she thought, and she chided herself for having promised to support Vince during his term as Club President.

As she was about to put away an unfinished bottle of

wine, the thought came into her mind, it would be nice to finish off the bottle while reading a book and having a nice long hot bath. She picked up the bottle and took a wine glass out of a kitchen cupboard. Slowly, almost dreamily, she moved through the house, checking the locks on the windows and doors and then went into their bedroom and on into its adjacent ensuite.

The ensuite was spacious, as big as the main bedroom in most walk-up flats found in the major cities. Passing a two-person shower cubicle with separate shower roses and taps, she skirted around a long white sunken spa bath big enough for two adults and two kids, and walked an extra couple of steps to reach an airing cupboard. She took out a folded bath towel and placed it on a small coffee table standing close to the wall opposite the bath, perhaps two metres distant.

Ilma carefully placed the bottle and the glass on the bath surround, turned on the hot tap, and added some bath salts to the water. She glanced around the room, taking in its contents. A marble vanity unit, a large wall mirror, two sets of heated towel rails, a cane chair, and a screened toilet recess. On the chair was a magazine, which she picked up and put on a small bath side table.

Satisfied everything was in order, Ilma returned to the bedroom and took off her clothes. She smiled as she thought about the panic Vincent would be in if he were to see her there in the nude, exposed for all through the uncovered window. He would be running over to draw the curtains, even though it was highly unlikely anyone would be trespassing in their back garden. Then she thought of Rod and how he might react. A little shiver ran through her. Leisurely, she went over to the bedside table and picked up a paperback edition of Alistair MacLeod's 'No Great Mischief', which she carried through to the en-suite and placed down next to the bottle of Clancy's Red. She turned on the cold tap and, because it would take a few moments to reduce water temperature to a level she could enter without scalding herself, she picked up the book again and sat in the cane chair reading the blurb on the back cover. When she had finished the last comment she put the book back next to the bottle, bent over the bath and dipped a finger into the water to test it. "Just a few seconds more," she murmured to herself, and then turned to look in the mirror.

Ilma was pleased at what she saw. Tennis and a weekly gym session had kept her body in good shape. Firm breasts, a flat stomach and smooth skin gave her the youthful appearance of a much younger woman. She struck a few poses, laughed and then gathered her hair up at the back and secured it with a couple of clips. She had another quick look in the mirror then tested the water again. Satisfied it was not too hot, she turned off the taps and stepped into the bath. She gently lowered herself into the water, relaxed for a few minutes and then poured a glass of wine.

As she sipped the wine she again wondered about Rod. She was pretty sure he would get in touch with her in Tamworth, and she wondered what she would do if he ever got serious. Part of her craved for the excitement of a new sexual experience and part of her wanted to remain loyal to Vincent. However, she did not see loyalty to Vincent in sexual terms. With Vincent it was more a question of giving him her support, keeping his house in order, encouraging him in his work and with his friends, and generally protecting his interests. Trying to make a life together really, this was what her marriage to Vincent is all about.

It was not her fault she often found life with Vincent to be a little bit of a bore, and she knew Vincent was just not capable of making it more exciting for her. Oh he is big, quite good looking, intelligent, generous, compassionate, and rock solid reliable, but she had never really been in love with him. When they first met it had hardly even been an infatuation, more a matter of point scoring over her contemporaries, enjoying the apparent sophistication of going out with an older man. She was too young and did not know how to retreat from the position in which she found herself. And there was not anyone else around anyway, well no one she thought was her equal, except perhaps for Brian, but he had been too interested in Jan. Maybe if she and Vincent had been able to have children she may feel less restless.

Ilma decided not to dwell on this and brought her mind back to Rod. She wondered if he would be at tennis tomorrow. She did not think so because he had asked her to give him a note at tomorrow night's dinner with Brian and Jan. She had found it hard work persuading Vincent they should go. She had been forced to tell him they had been specially invited, whereas the truth was she had rung Jan and asked her if they could join them. Regardless, she would be pleased to see Rod if he did turn up at the tennis club, and she would try not to complain at having to go to yet another club dinner, even with Brian and Jan, who at least made her laugh.

A vision of Rod came to her. She imagined him in the en-suite, standing there with his dark eyes looking down at her, sweeping along her body as she lay there, and closing in on her face. Despite the bath water heat, another little shiver went through her. She shook her head and decided it was time to read her book. She poured another glass of wine and picked up her book. She took a sip of wine and then put the book down again. Whatever mischief lie within its pages would not be as exciting as the mischief she could contemplate as she thought about Rod.

★

Making news, Saturday 22 February 1997:
The third annual Screen Actors Guild was held today. Category winners include Geoffrey Rush, Frances McDermond, Dennis Franz and Gillian Anderson.

Comment:
A number of people at a certain party in Sandhaven Creek may have been talking about this news item, since a Geoffrey Rush film was currently showing at the local cinema. However, Best Actor award should have been given to Vincent Mathews, who put on a star performance for the benefit of his wife.

Ilma was still in bed when Vincent brought her breakfast into the room on a tray. A small gift-wrapped parcel and an envelope rested beside the two soft boiled eggs, the toast, the butter pats, and the teacup.

"Happy birthday, dear," said Vincent, as he put the tray in front of her, gave her a quick kiss and then sat on the edge of the bed.

Ilma eagerly opened the envelope, took out the card and read it. She opened the parcel to reveal a small oblong box. "It could be a necklace or a watch," she thought. Inside she found a pair of sunglasses with bright red frames. Finding it hard to hide her disappointment, Ilma removed them from the box and tried them on. She thought the sunglasses looked a bit cheap and said coldly, "Oh, nice, thank you." She put the sunglasses down on the bedside table.

Ilma looked so disconcerted Vincent wondered if he should tell her the glasses were only a token gift and he had yet to pick up the real present. However he realised this would only make complications, and may even give the game away. Instead, he gave her a quick kiss on the forehead and told her he had to go to a committee meeting at the social club and would be back well before lunch, and in plenty of time to take her to tennis.

After he had gone, Ilma picked up the sunglasses and had a closer look at them. They still look cheap, she thought, and what on earth possessed him to buy them anyway. He knows I already have a perfectly good pair. I suppose they actually cost a lot of money but I still don't like them. She put them back on the bedside table, next to the alarm clock. She saw it is still only eight thirty, so she finished her breakfast, pushed the tray well out of her way, turned on her side, and went back to sleep.

It was nearly eleven o'clock when she re-awoke to the sound of a telephone ringing. She had been in a deep sleep and it took her a few moments to gather her wits together and pick up the phone. Putting the receiver to her ear she whispered, "Ilma Mathews speaking." She heard a click and the phone go dead.

A wrong number, or could it have been Rod, she wondered. She chided herself for sleeping in. She waited for a while but the phone didn't ring again. Realising the time, she jumped into the shower before Vincent returned.

Later, at approximately six o'clock in the evening, Ilma was waiting for Vincent to get ready to take her to the club bistro. She was pondering what to say to Rod, and how to slip him a card with the gallery address and telephone number on it. While waiting, she poured herself a gin and tonic, which she felt she needed. Vincent seemed to be taking a bit longer than usual to get changed, and she wondered if he had perhaps hurt himself a little bit more than he had let on when he got up after falling at tennis. Her conscience was starting to prick her. She realised she could have been a little more sympathetic, but then it had not been a very good day. She had felt quite depressed when they got to tennis and found Rod was not there, and nor was Sally. Ilma worried about this. Had she been mistaken about Rod and Sally, was there something more going on between them than she had first thought?

When Ilma had arrived at tennis Jan wished her a happy birthday and gave her a small gift, but there was no further reference from Vincent to the fact it was her birthday, and she derived no joy from losing three sets of tennis. So it is perhaps understandable her present mood is somewhere on the dark side of sombre. Vincent had better be ready soon or he can go to the bloody social club on his own, she thought, and then chided herself because she knew she would go with him because she still wanted to see Rod again.

She sat back, trying to relax. Her gaze wandered around the room and eventually settled on her old fencing foil, hanging on the wall. She had kept it all these years, hopeful she would one day again take up fencing, but she had found no interest in the sport in Sandhaven Creek, and nor was she likely to. Vincent hadn't seen her fencing, it was before his time, and she had never told him, or anyone else in Sandhaven Creek, about Maximilian.

She mentally pictured Maximilian and thought how he and Rod were so alike to look at, but she hoped Rod would prove to be more generous in nature.

On her third sip of sherry, the telephone rang. Ilma sighed, picked up the handpiece and responded to the call.

"Ilma Mathews, speaking."

"Hi Ilma, it's Jan. I'm sooo glad to find you're still at home. You aren't going to believe this but, oh, Brian's car has a flat battery and I picked up a puncture on the way home from tennis, and my spare's a dud. Brian's rung the Road Service but they're flat out and cannot get anyone here under a couple of hours. So I wondered if you can pick us up? We're supposed to be meeting Rod in the foyer at seven thirty to sign him in."

"Yes, of course, Jan. Vincent isn't quite ready yet but

he shouldn't be much longer. I think his knee may have stiffened up after falling at tennis."

"Gosh, I saw him fall. I was on the next court. He was going pretty fast at the time, how is he?"

"Oh, he may be a bit sore but he'll live. Hold on a minute, He has just closed the bedroom door, and I can hear him coming now. Vince, it's Jan, they have car troubles, can we pick them up in half an hour? They're supposed to meet Rod at seven thirty, good, yes Jan, okay, see you shortly."

Jan's reference to meeting Rod came as a relief to Ilma, for on first hearing Jan speak, she had feared it might mean dinner was cancelled. Her mood brightened, but despite her guilty conscience, or perhaps because of it, she was still down on Vincent for buying her such a lousy birthday present. Vincent entered the room. Looking at him she said, "You took your time, anything wrong?"

Vincent was not put out hearing the sharpness in her voice. He knew he was in the doghouse. Usually, if anything untoward happened to him Ilma will display plenty of sympathy. However earlier today, when he fell over at tennis and his knee was bleeding, she had uncharacteristically shown very little concern.

Satisfied Ilma's mood related to his recent deceptions, Vincent ignored her petulantly spoken words and replied to the question. Calmly he said, "No. Not really. I had to clean my knee up a bit, it got some court grit in it. I bathed it in Dettol and put on the biggest Band Aid you've ever seen over. Should be okay now, just a little stiff. Are you ready to go?"

"Yes, I've been waiting for you. Haven't you got a better shirt to put on?"

★

On the drive over to Brian's house, Ilma was quiet. Vincent understood how she would have been disappointed with the sunglasses for he had only paid five dollars for them at the local imports shop, and he knew also she did not have a very good day at tennis, because she liked to win. So he could relate to Ilma's silence and he didn't want to inflame her mood before they got to Brian's house.

When they got there, Vincent was relieved to see there were no cars parked nearby. He pulled into Brian's driveway, left the car and rang Brian's doorbell. Brian opened the door, said a few words to Vincent and then ushered him inside. The door remained slightly open.

Ilma sat in the car, with the window open, fiddling with the clasp on her small evening bag while waiting. After five minutes passed, she began to fume. Then Jan appeared in the open doorway and calls, "Hi there Ilma, come in and have a drink. Rod's just called, he's delayed, may be up to half an hour he said. Brian is taking the opportunity to get back to the Road Service and arrange for them to bring a new battery over in the morning."

Well, thought Ilma, her heartbeat lifting, the day might not be a total loss. At least Rod is still coming to the club. She opened the car door and called back, "What a good idea. Actually I had a drink before we started out, but it's been one of those days and I'm actually ready for another one." She got out of the car and joined Jan.

At the doorstep she stopped to admire a new plant pot, wanting to talk about it. Jan managed to discourage the conversation and bustled her into the house.

Inside, and mid way along a wide hallway, Brian was standing beside a small table. He had a telephone receiver in his hand and a finger on the connection button. "I still can't get through," he said, nodding towards them, then, "hello Ilma, Vince is in the lounge, go on in."

Ilma was familiar with their house layout – two large interconnecting living areas, each with a doorway off the hallway. The first space was used as a lounge and the second space served for formal dining. Ilma opened the first door and a very loud chorus of 'Happy Birthday' greeted her. She was momentarily stunned before bursting into tears of emotion. Everything and everyone in front of her was blurred for a moment before things became clear and she took it all in. A big HAPPY BIRTHDAY banner was pinned above the wide opening between the two rooms and several bundles of balloons hung from the ceiling. A blue cardboard backed frieze of photographs depicting her life ran almost the entire length of one wall and sitting on the large coffee table were gifts in wrappings of various colours and textures.

She recognised Vincent's handwriting on one of many gift cards. Straight away she realised the sunglasses he had given her at breakfast time were only a trick.

Vincent was standing beside the coffee table, holding a glass of champagne out towards her. She blurted out, "Oh my gawd, oh my gawd Vince, you sly old devil," and gave him a kiss while accepting the proffered glass.

A number of camera lights flashed. The cameras all belonged to friends, except for the one in the hands of Phillip Jackson, the eighteen year old professional photographer, who survived largely on pictures he sold to the Journal. Ilma remembered it was he who took the tennis team photo, after they won the women's pennant trophy last year.

Another flash went off and lit up the table. Ilma's attention was drawn to the large amount of food sitting on the table. She went over to Jan and asked, "Did you do all this, Jan?" and without waiting for confirmation she gave her a hug. She saw Brian standing in the doorway. Grinning, she called out, "And you, Brian, I suppose your car hasn't got a flat battery has it? Boy, did you guys fool me."

Jillian Parker, and Sam and Betty Isherwood, caught her attention to offer their best wishes, while other guests awaited their turn and carried on their interrupted conversations.

It was not long before Florian came over to her. She could tell he had already had a few drinks. He was dressed in worn and not too clean looking blue jeans, with a yellow and red vertically striped long sleeved shirt, and a navy blue cravat. His cheeks were flushed and his pale blue eyes had red flecks on the corners. He pushed his small but portly frame forward until he was only a foot short of being chest to breast with her.

"Dolly, Dolly," he said in a booming voice. "You don't look more than twenty-one. I must get around to painting your portrait." He turned and poked his finger into Vincent's tummy. "Vincent, tell Ilma she must come and sit for me," he said, trying to take over the conversation, but Brian interfered.

"Come Florian, let's move over to the table, Sally and Jan have put on this terrific buffet and we've all been standing around looking at it, and I don't know about you but my mouth is watering, and my stomach is empty, so come on and let's start eating." Ilma and Jan gave him a grateful look as he took hold of Florian's arm and gently but forcefully propelled him towards the table.

Ilma looked at Jan. "Did Sally cook some of this?" she asked.

Jan smiled, "Did Sally do some of this, well you could say so, but you'd be wrong. Actually, she has just about done all of it, she took over my kitchen this afternoon. She loves cooking you know, she sometimes comes early for dinner, and then cooks it for us while Brian and I get out into the garden or whatever."

So, thought Ilma. This is why Sally was not at tennis. With a sense of relief she decided she could now enjoy the party.

Expectantly, she went looking for Rod. She soon found him talking to Contessa Ralstone. It didn't bother her, even though Contessa was strikingly good looking. She was undoubtedly a good conversationalist, but with men she didn't seem to have any urge to go beyond talking. Ilma was starting to think she was probably lesbian.

"Hello Contessa," she said. "Keep on the right side of this man and you may get us some good publicity. Has he told you he's the Ace Reporter on the Journal, and probably Sandhaven Creek's one and only art critic?"

Contessa laughed. "Actually, I've been telling him

about your gallery, and I may have even persuaded him to do an article on it one day."

They discussed the gallery and some of its artists and then Rod, on cue, asked, "Where exactly is this gallery, I mean, does it have an address?"

Ilma reached into her evening bag and took out a visiting card. "Here you are," she said, "Dareboolah is only a small place, it's easy to find the gallery, but it's best if you ring first because we vary the opening hours sometimes, depending on the weather and the number of people about, and you wouldn't want to go there at the wrong time, would you?"

Ilma could see from Rod's face the message had got home, and she was pretty certain Contessa had not twigged its real meaning.

They continued to talk until Vincent called out, "Thank you, thank you, time for the party girl to open her presents." He had a strong voice and a commanding presence. Everyone stopped talking and looked his way, and he continued, "Will everyone gather around please." Motioning towards Ilma he said, "Come on Ilma love, over here near the goodies, but we want a speech from you before you're allowed to open any presents."

Ilma was mortified, she hated speechmaking, and she self-consciously went over to stand beside Vincent. He had picked up a present and was holding it, ready to give to her. She could see the wrapping had a glossy birthday card attached with the message 'Happy birthday to my dear wife' printed in gold letters. Poor Vincent, she thought, he has to be the team leader and be seen to be doing the right thing. Why couldn't he have just given her the present, and why didn't he buy a card which said something more intimate, or was even daringly funny?

Ilma took a deep breath and made a short speech. "Wow," she started. "How do you make a speech when you're speechless? This really has been a surprise. Thank you all very much for coming and thanks to Brian and Jan for the use of their lovely home, and thanks to Sally, who I understand was the party chef. It's delicious food, thank you Sally, I wondered why you were absent from tennis. And of course, thank you too Vince, you really had me fooled." She paused then says, "Can I open my presents now?"

After unwrapping the presents, Ilma felt obliged to go on a thank-you tour. Throughout the evening she was unable to get more than a few moments alone with Rod. There always seemed to be someone standing next to him, and she knew it would be unwise to be seen to be following him around. She was annoyed at not being able to be alone with him. But after a few drinks her mood gradually changed as she, from time to time, caught glimpses of him in the party crowd. She became thrilled at the thought of what might eventuate if they did get time together.

Much later, when she and Vincent were on their way home, she touched Vincent on the arm and said, "Thanks Vince, thanks again. It was a very nice idea. A lovely surprise." However she knew she still wanted to have a sexual adventure with Rod, and the only thing changed was, she now felt guilty about it.

5
Rod Meets Beryl

Making news, Thursday 27 February 1997:
Today marks the official recognition of divorce in the Irish Republic.

Comment:
Rod Skapleson heard the news on his car radio and gave a chuckle, "Not before time," he said out loud. Vincent Mathews heard the subject being discussed in the school staff room. He was disappointed with the popular view of his staff which supported the decision, for he firmly believed in the sanctity of marriage. Sally Tully, an avid newspaper reader, saw the reference on page three and gave a sigh.

Thursday afternoon. The temperature was about thirty degrees and the sky was clear of cloud for as far as Rod can see. He was sitting behind the wheel of a two year old Golf Cabriolet he had bought, the day after leaving Melbourne and ending it with Norma. He was on his way to pick up the week's advertising copy from the Journal's Tamworth Agent, and to attend and report on the Tamworth Harness Club race meeting. He, of course, also intended to get in touch with Ilma and try to foster what promised to become an exciting, if short, relationship.

He remembered Ilma asking him if he was on the run from an ex-girlfriend, and he had replied there was an ex-girlfriend, but she was three years ex. He was glad Ilma had not pressed the question of him being on the run, and he smiled to himself as his thoughts continue. I wonder what she would say if I told her I was. I suppose it wouldn't matter if she knew about Penny because it was actually nearer to four years ago, and we were only living together a couple of weeks. But, Norma? Well, I don't think I'll crack on about Norma. A wife can be a bit more off-putting than an ex-girlfriend, particularly if the wife is not legally ex.

Rod negotiated a sharp bend then continued to reminisce. He wondered what Norma had been up to. Probably got herself another promotion at the bank. She had been too interested in her career. So busy trying to make money, she didn't have time to live. Maybe she did contribute nearly all the money for the house deposit, and okay, she had put the most money into their savings account, but what sort of life had they been having? Running around in a sixteen year old car which was ready for the wreckers, still using his old Toshiba T.V., an almost pre-historic model and certainly pre the development of remote controls, trying to hold barbecues with a ridiculous little three legged coke burner, and him spending all of his weekends and most of his evenings restoring the garden and renovating the house. And all because she had insisted a tumble-down timber cottage in an inner Melbourne suburb would be a good investment. Yeah, well she can sell it now, or finish doing it up herself, he thought. If she wants to sell it, all she has to do is give the sale contract papers to Andrew to pass on to me, and I'll sign them quick as a flash.

The note Rod put next to the kitchen phone said it all: Goodbye. You won't see me, again, life with you is too hard. I am going interstate so don't bother looking for me. Keep the house, or sell it, or burn it down if you want. If you need anything signed see Andrew, I'll be keeping in touch with him. Sorry, but I have emptied the savings account. I have had to buy a few things, including a decent car.

Rod had to leave Norma. They could never have had a life together. Their relationship was full of jealousy. He couldn't even glance at another woman, let alone talk to one. And she was nagging all the time. We must do this or we must do the other, but this or the other was always something to do with house improvements or getting on in the world, and never about enjoying life.

Hell! I'm only twenty-six, he thought. I don't want to be tied down to anyone. The marriage was a big mistake, all her idea. She dangled the carrot of a bit of money in the bank, and I fell for it, hook, line and sinker. She didn't tell me it was all going to go on a house deposit. We could have been living it up for a while, maybe a few years in London or Paris. But no. Not Norma.

Needing the support of his brother, Rod told Andrew of his intention a couple of weeks before actually leaving Norma. Andrew had always looked out for Rod and had earlier warned him about Norma, saying she would put a lot of pressure on a man. Rod told him he had secretly gotten another job and asked him not to tell Norma where he was but to keep him informed about her reaction. Good old Andrew, it was a big ask, but he had agreed.

He approached the Dareboolah turn off and was tempted to go into Dareboolah and drive past the gallery just to get a feel for the place, but he was running a little bit late so he decided to head on towards Tamworth. Then, with the Dareboolah turn off a few miles behind him, he returned to his reverie.

Yes, Andrew is a good brother, he thought. He had been perceptive enoughto know Rod was not happy as a carpenter, and it was he who suggested he tried his hand at journalism. Andrew had engineered a job for Rod with 'The Builders Guide'. Only a trade journal, but it did give Rod a good start in journalism, even if Norma thought the pay was lousy. Still, he learnt a lot in those two years at The Guide, and they did give him a good reference when he told them he was leaving.

I don't suppose I would have got the Journal job if it had not been for the reference, he thought. Rod had pretended to Joe Bernaldo that he had been with the Melbourne Herald for a couple of years before working at The Guide. He doubted Joe would bother to telephone the Herald office since he already had such a good reference from The Guide. Of course he wouldn't have lied to him if he had not thought it necessary in order to get the job. As it turned out, he would have got the job anyway because there were no other applicants. He quite liked Joe. They worked well together. Maybe one day he could set the record straight with him.

Rod ended his reverie and slowed the car to conform with the sixty kilometre speed limit sign which he was approaching.

Shortly he saw another sign which said: 'Welcome to Tamworth, the Country Music Capital. Population thirty-five thousand.'

Gradually, Rod became aware the traffic had increased as he entered the town's outskirts. It was a much bigger town than he had imagined. He passed through the suburb of Westdale and travelled on, going first past Dampier Street which led to the racecourse, and then the Gunnedah Road which led to the greyhound club and the showgrounds. He turned left into Creek Road and on into Bridge Street, then through West Tamworth, across the Peel River bridge and into the town centre. He found a parking place opposite to the Police and Community Youth Club buildings. Carrying a briefcase, he walked along Peel Street until he reached Bebe Eisler's Newsagency. A notice in the window stated: 'Advertising copy for the Sandhaven and District Journal can be submitted here'.

Rod entered the shop and talked to Bebe for a while. When he returned to his car he had two new sealed envelopes in his briefcase. One filled with submissions for next week's classified, and the other containing a transactions statement and a cheque.

Rod took an address card from his pocket and read it: Beryl Thomas, Fig Tree House B and B, 43 Bridge St., Tamworth. He memorised the street number and returned the card to his pocket.

Rod drove there, looked around for a moment and

decided he liked the place. He entered the building, went to the reception counter and pressed the bell. It rang but no one answered. After a while he gave it another ring, with the same result. Becoming impatient, he decided to explore. He walked down a corridor, past a few numbered doors, and headed towards the corridor end. Facing him was a sand-blasted glass panelled door, with a printed sign advising it was the entrance to the dining room. He opened the door.

Inside there were eight tables, each with two chairs. A small slim neatly dressed woman, who looked to Rod to be about forty years of age, was standing near a service trolley piled with dishes and cutlery. A radio standing on a sideboard was throwing out some rather loud rhythm music and the woman was swaying to it as she placed knives and forks on the table nearest to her. For a moment she was unaware of Rod's presence. She danced a full turn and picked up some more knives and forks, and in so doing saw Rod. She stopped dancing and stood there looking a bit flustered.

Rod looked at her. Thinking she was quite good looking, he wondered if she was there every day, and whether she would be serving at breakfast. "Sorry to startle you," he said. "Are you Beryl Thomas?"

The woman looked at him as she took a few steps backwards and turned the radio volume down. She smiled and replied to his question.

"Yes. I'm Beryl Thomas. Sorry, I didn't hear you. I like a bit of good music while I'm setting the tables. Now, what can I do for you?"

Rod took in her friendly face and her youthful figure and blonde hair. He thought she could do quite a lot for him. "Hi Beryl, I'm Rod Skapleson, the new reporter with the Journal."

"Oh yes, I was expecting you," she acknowledged, extending her hand towards him in greeting, and grasping Rod's hand very firmly. "You don't look a bit like your predecessor," she continued. "He looked very unkempt and in poor health. I used to feel quite sorry for him." Slowly she released Rod's hand, and he felt it tingle from the pressure of her grip, then, in a bright clear voice conveying openness she said, "The room Tom had has been taken, but I do have a couple of rooms which have just been renovated. They are behind the main building and only accessible from the garden path. They have proved to be unsuitable for my permanents who are mostly older people. I'm about to advertise them as bed and breakfast holiday accommodation, which is a new venture for me. I imagine most demand will be for weekend visits, so I could let you have one for Thursday nights I suppose, providing you keep paying me in advance."

"I am told you serve a good breakfast. Do you provide any other meals?"

"No, I'm afraid not. I work seven days so I like my evenings free. Would you like to see the two rooms? At the moment you can have your choice of either. It is quicker if we go out through the door over there, which, I prefer to keep locked over night. I don't want to open it before seven o'clock, unless you make a special request for an earlier breakfast, and for an earlier breakfast I'll be charging extra."

Rod nodded. "I can see you're a businesswoman," he said with a grin as they walked through the doorway to the driveway beside the house.

"But only a fair one," she replied.

Yes, I believe she is, he thinks, while experiencing a strange feeling of trust towards her. It is as if they were always meant to become friends and to understand each other. Apart from Andrew he had never really trusted anyone before, and he wondered why he felt this way towards Beryl. In the few minutes he had been in her company their relationship had already changed. She was certainly womanly, yet he no longer saw her as a sex object. There was something about her which made him respect her, and yet in her presence he felt relaxed. And this was a very new experience for Rod.

While they walked along the driveway, Rod asked Beryl if he would be able to have a key to the dining room door as he didn't fancy walking all the way to the reception entrance if it were raining. Beryl advised him she was considering making keys available to the B&B guests, but would be asking for a deposit on the keys, to ensure their return. In a friendly voice she explained she meant no offence to him, but she couldn't put the building security at risk, and asking for a key deposit would have to be a house rule for everyone.

They followed a path beside the building. Rounding the building corner Rod saw a single-storey wing with the two rooms. Beryl opened the door to the first room and they both entered. Rod liked it straight away, but then he thought of something. "What about a telephone," he said. "There doesn't appear to be one."

"Not a problem," answered Beryl. "The connection for the two rooms has just been installed. Look, down there near the bedside table under the window. The handsets are being delivered in the morning." She smiled and made a fingers crossed sign.

Rod wandered around, looked in the en-suite, opened cupboards, and then sat on the bed. "Anything in the fridge?" he asked.

"Not yet. I'll stock it as soon as I get my first guest."

"Well, the room looks fine. Did you pick the colours?"

Beryl laughed. "I not only picked them but I did all the painting myself. It took me ages."

"How did you find the time? Do you have any staff?"

"Only Sylvia. She does the rooms every day and washes up after breakfast. There's another girl, Polly, comes at the weekends. The cooking I do myself."

Rod got up and went over to look at a small bench-top microwave in the kitchenette area. He fiddled with the microwave controls, satisfied that he can operate it properly. Beryl stood watching him. Curious, he asked, "How long have you had the place?"

"Oh, let me see," said Beryl. "Harry and I bought it about fifteen years ago. It was pretty run down at the time. Harry did the renovation work and I was the follow-up painter. It was two years before we opened for business."

"And Harry is your husband? I mean he's not just a business partner?"

"No." Beryl paused and then quietly continued. "Harry passed away five years back. We were married the year before we found the place. We bought it with Harry's inheritance. He went suddenly, you know. He had a second heart attack. He shouldn't have been out digging in the garden, but he was a proud and stubborn man who liked his garden to be just right."

Beryl gave a little sigh. "I'm over it now," she said, in a slightly stronger voice.

Rod looked at her. "I'm sorry. It must have been hard for you. I'll take this room if it's alright with you, I'll need a dining room key, and I need to make a phone call. Is there a phone I can use?"

"Yes, there's one at reception. I am pleased you like the room, Rod. Don't worry about the pay phone, use the one behind the counter. I'll be in the dining room when you've finished."

Rod had made no reference to Ilma in his conversation with Beryl, although he intuitively knew that he had found a friend and confidante in her. If she were to ask if he had a girlfriend he would probably say yes, and if she pressed him for details he would want to be open with her and tell her he was really just playing up to Ilma's advances, and nothing serious was involved. Nevertheless, he found it hard to break a lifetime habit of secretiveness, and was very mindful of Vincent's size and his influence within Sandhaven Creek, he saw no reason to unnecessarily volunteer such dangerous information.

Rod made his way back to the reception, and rang the number Ilma had given him.

He heard her voice answer.

"Hello, Ilma Mathews speaking."

"Hi, are you alone?"

"Oh. Hi Gypsy Boy. Yes, I am alone. Where are you?"

"I'm in Tamworth. I'll be tied up tonight at the race meeting. Perhaps we can have coffee somewhere in the morning?"

"Ooo, Yes. There's a nice little place in Peel Street, near the viaduct crossing. It has the ridicules name of 'Cuckoo Coffee Cups'. You'll see why when we get there. Say ten o'clock?"

"Okay. I have to go. I'm in a hurry."

"Wait. What's your phone number at the hotel?"

"I'm staying at a private hotel in Bridge Street. No telephone in my room until tomorrow. It's a long story."

"Well, where are you ringing from now?"

"I'm using a house phone. I don't want you to ring me on it. I'll explain in the morning. Wear something sexy."

★

Later, installed in his room, Rod decided to have a meat pie and some chips at the race club canteen. He checked his briefcase, took out all its contents and placed them on the bed. From the pile he picked up the two envelopes, his cheque book, the Journal's cheque book, and his wallet, and put them on the bedside cabinet. He placed the Journal's current lift-out racing guide, two notebooks, a spare biro pen, and a sheaf of handwritten notes back into the briefcase. Stuffing the wallet into his pocket, he looked around for a safe hiding place for the envelopes and the cheque books. He noticed the stubby little legs of the bedside cabinet which lifted the base about fifty millimetres above the carpet. With a bit of effort he moved the cabinet, put the envelopes and the cheque books on the carpet in the space where the cabinet originally stood, and then moved the cabinet back into its original position.

There was a knock on the door. He opened it to find Beryl, with a basket of goodies to put in the fridge and bench-top containers. She sorted them out and asked what time she could expect him for breakfast. He suggested eight o'clock, and she thanked him and departed. He could see she was very efficient.

Satisfied the valuables were well hidden, breakfast arrangements were in hand, and coffee and biscuits were available for supper, he set out for the race track.

6
Deceit in Dareloobah

Making news, Friday 28 February 1997:
Stone tools, believed to date back 300,000 years, have been found near Yakutsk, in Siberia. Scientists are surprised that primitives could have existed so close to the Arctic Circle at such an early date.

Comment:
In discussing this subject at home over coffee with his wife, Brian Clements questioned if scientists had been able to accurately determine the earth's average temperature, for any relatively short period of time so long ago. Perhaps, he suggested, the Arctic region may have actually had a temperate climate lasting only a few hundred years, and during this period the primitives stayed around. "Things are not always as they seem," he commented. Meanwhile, two other people having coffee away from home discussed a very different subject.

Friday morning. Ilma sat at a table on the pavement outside the Cuckoo Coffee Cups coffee shop, waiting for Rod. She was wearing pink slacks and a yellow halter top. The slacks were tight around her hips and loose on the legs and finished at mid calf length. They showed off her well-

Fred Wyke

rounded bottom and, since she was sitting with her legs crossed, revealed a good proportion of shapely bare leg. Several passing men had looked her way with lingering glances.

They'd had plenty of time to do so, since she'd been waiting now for over twenty minutes and had already consumed one cup of coffee. Rod was not late, because it was not yet ten o'clock. However, Ilma had been unable to contain her excitement and had chosen to be at the coffee shop well before the appointed time. Just in case he was early.

She was very nervous and trying hard not to show it.

Across the road she saw the red V.W. pull into a car parking space. She watched as Rod got out, locked the car and walked towards the coffee shop. She found his loose, almost panther-like, walk to be quite sensual. As he side stepped to avoid a passing vehicle, she related his display of grace and agility to that of a Spanish bullfighter. A fleeting image of him in full Matador costume, complete with cloak and sword, came to her mind – almost expecting him to bow when he reached the table.

He stood there for a moment, looking down at her. He was wearing sunglasses and she couldn't see his eyes. "You look nice," he said. "Sorry if I'm a bit late. I had some unexpected work to do."

How nice, she thought. He was not late, he was just being polite she was already there. She smiled at him and went along with it.

"Well, it's okay then. Now we can kiss and make up." She tilted her head back and pouted her lips.

"My, my. In broad daylight," Rod said, and gave her a light kiss on the cheek. He took a seat opposite to her and continued, "You're incorrigible." He grinned, "Don't you know half of Tamworth is looking at you?"

"What, this early on a Friday morning. It's not likely there will be anyone around who knows both of us. How are you? And what sort of place are you staying at, which doesn't provide you with a telephone?"

Rod wondered for a moment whether to divulge his address, then deciding there will not be any harm in it, he said, "A big red house in Bridge Street. It's a sort of private hotel. There are a couple of rooms at the back which have just been renovated. I'm in one of those.

Rod eased back in his chair and took off his sunglasses. Ilma could see he was looking directly at her as he continued, "A woman named Beryl Thomas owns the place. A good-looking blonde," he added mischievously.

Ilma noticed the glint in his eye when he said this, and realised he was teasing her. She decided to tease him back. "So, whatever attracted you to staying there?" she asked. "As if I couldn't guess."

Rod laughed. "Well actually, it was Beryl, but not for the reason you are imagining. Our Tamworth agent, Bebe Eisler, recommended the place. Said Beryl provides a good breakfast."

Ilma was satisfied with the by-play between them. She carried on. "And does she?" she asked.

"Yes, if this morning is any indication. Bacon, eggs, fried tomato, the lot."

"And what happened to the phones?"

"Oh. The room renovations have just finished. The phones are being installed today."

The arrival of a waitress interrupted the conversation. She picked up Ilma's empty cup and they ordered two more coffees, a cappuccino for Ilma, and a long black for Rod. The waitress left and Ilma started up the conversation again. She reached across the table and held Rod's hand.

"I feel good sitting here with you, Rod," she said, without any sign of embarrassment. "It's as if it was meant to be. I can't believe I feel so happy. I mean, I'm aware I'm married and I know Vincent is a good man who deserves better from me, but just at this moment, now we're together, it doesn't seem to matter."

"Must be my aftershave," said Rod, trying to hide his embarrassment with a joke.

Ilma laughed. "No. It's not your aftershave you silly goose. You know it's much more." Yes, she thought. It was a lot more than the aftershave. He had an inner captured energy, tight held like a stalking cat. Energy, ready to be triggered at will. It gave her the shivers, yet attracted her like hell. And then there were his eyes, and their lazy lids. Thinking eyes, suggestive eyes – eyes to victimise her with.

She smiled to herself and her voice became dreamy, she turned Rod's hand over and studied his palm. "I wish I was a palmist and could tell your fortune. I hope you're going to have a happy life, Rod. I really do," she said, fastening her gaze back on his face.

Rod looked at her and his expression softened. "Well," he said in a firm voice. "I'm very happy now, and I'd rather not know about the future. I like to take things a day at a time."

"Don't you ever dream?"

"No. I'm more interested in going with the flow. Like now, for instance. I mean, why would I want to dream when I'm already sitting here with a gorgeous looking girl?"

Ilma accepted the compliment and sighed. "Yes, but we can't stay here for ever."

"You're right you know. So when we've finished our coffee, what comes next?"

"Oh, all sorts of things I hope, Rod. It depends on how much free time you have. When do you have to be back in Sandhaven Creek?"

"Well, there's a bit of a problem here. I'm normally back before midday, and then I help make up the advertising copy. We get everything except the weekend news made up before we close for business on Fridays. This means we only have the weekend news and sport results to put together on Monday before going to press."

Rod knew what they both wanted, but needed Ilma to spell it out. Choosing his words carefully, he continued, "So if we're going to spend some time together it'll have to be like this on Friday mornings, or you can come to the race meetings, or we can spend the night together on Thursdays. It's up to you. You have to realise I'm in Tamworth to work. Best I can do if you don't want me to spend the night with you, is get here a bit earlier on Thursdays, but I don't want to share you with some budding artists?"

"What time do the races start, Rod?"

"First race is at 7.30 but I have to be there at least half

an hour before to check through the running lists."

"Mmm. Not much time there, sometimes I'm stuck with an artist until seven o'clock. What time does the meeting end?"

"It's a seven-race programme so it finishes at ten thirty. I get away at about eleven."

"So you could be at the gallery at say eleven thirty?"

"If you want me to, yes."

Ilma was unhappy with the way the conversation was going. Rod's available time seemed to be very limited. The dreaminess left her voice and it became brittle.

"Well I do, Rod," she said sharply. "You don't think I've gone to all this trouble for nothing, do you? I mean, there's a limit to how we can relate just sitting in a coffee shop, particularly if you're too scared to give me a proper kiss in public. And although I don't mind occasionally going to a race meeting it wouldn't be much different there, would it? And we cannot freely meet in Sandhaven Creek, so?"

"You're right, of course." Rod paused, knowing he has achieved his objective and there is no need for him to hold back any longer. "Look," he says, "I took the room in Bridge Street as it has a separate entrance. I can enter at any time without disturbing anyone. I can stay at your place overnight, leave the gallery early in the morning before our little township wakes up, and be back at Bridge Street for breakfast without anyone being the wiser as to where I've been. So."

There was another interruption to the conversation as the coffee was served. Then Rod continued. "So, how does it sound?"

Ilma's mood changed again, her face lighting up.

"Ooo, sounds wicked," she laughed. "And will you bring your pyjamas? I'll bet they're bright red."

"I'm not telling. You'll find out when I come."

Rod looked at the coffee cups and pulled a face. The cups were weirdly shaped, both hideously coloured with lime, orange, yellow or blue wavy lines painted all over them. He picked up his cup and sipped at the coffee. "Thank God the coffee is better than the cups," he remarked.

They sat looking at each other for a few moments then Ilma reached over and put her hand on his. Her eyes were a bit moist as she looked at him and said, "I'm looking forward to next Thursday, Gypsy. You don't mind me calling you Gypsy, do you?"

Rid found it embarrassing and a bit childish. He let the question pass and said nothing. He didn't want to spoil things – the future looked far too promising.

Ilma continued, "Apart from the caravan there's a little bit of Gypsy in you, isn't there? I think it is why I find you so attractive. You're a wanderer. A man of mystery. I wish you and I could get up and wander off together, right now. But I know it isn't possible. I'll be waiting for you next Thursday though. I just want you to know how I really feel."

Rod smiled at her. She was getting to be more serious than he would have liked, he thought. Although she wasn't a woman blessed with a beautiful or even pretty face, there was, in her eyes, a certain vitality which he found attractive. And sitting there, in her tight at the hips pants and her halter top, he saw her as too desirable to give up so soon.

"Well, you know about Gypsies, Ilma. They come and they go. I'm here now, and I will be next week. Let's just take it a day at a time, huh? You're fun and I'm free. We may spoil what we have if we start making problems, huh?"

Ilma kept hold of his hand while she replied. "I know, Rod. I know. I'm just having my little dream. We'll enjoy it while we can."

Slowly Ilma withdrew her hand and dropped her gaze. Then quietly she asked, "What about tomorrow. Will you be at tennis?"

"Unless some big news breaks in Sandhaven Creek. Which I think is unlikely."

"We'll have to be careful."

"Yes. I think it'll be best if we try not to play together. I don't fancy a punch on the nose from Vincent. He's quite a big boy."

"Don't, Rod. I feel guilty enough."

Rod frowned and looked across the road. "Is it Florian, over there, near the chemist?"

"Christ, yes. I hope he doesn't come this way. Maybe we should go." Ilma felt for her handbag. "I'll pay. You just go, Gypsy." She got up, gave Rod a quick kiss and headed towards the shop counter. Rod put on his sunglasses. He gave her a big grin and quickly walked towards his car, calling back, "See you Thursday. I'll ring you before the races start."

Hiding in the shop, Ilma kept an eye on Florian. He had stopped to talk with a rather large woman who Ilma recognises as an assistant in the Chemist's shop. A would-be artist who once brought some dreadfully amateurish paintings to the gallery for display, and had to be told they were not up to standard. Ilma saw her as a dangerous woman – a woman who could become spiteful.

She continued to watch them. Florian was typically animated, throwing his arms around while talking, and obviously a little bit under the influence, even though it was not yet lunch time. From the corner of her eye she saw Rod's car take off and she sighed with relief. Florian patted the woman on the shoulder as if encouraging her and then, with an unsteady gait, he walked away in the opposite direction

Ilma paid for the coffee, returned to her car and sat in it for a while. Seeing Florian and the shop assistant woman had unsettled her and she needed time to calm down. The risk she was taking in having an affair with Rod had suddenly become very real and she did not want to blow her marriage to Vincent, with all the care and comfort it provided. She must, she thought, avoid any unnecessary contact with Rod in Sandhaven Creek, and, in particular, try not to make any signs to him at the tennis club. She would have to be extra nice to Vincent and try to overcome her guilty feelings.

Meanwhile, Rod turned onto the highway and relaxed his attention to the traffic as it became less dense. He was thinking about Ilma and what it would be like sleeping with an older woman.

★

Making news, Thursday 6 March 1997:
Queen Elizabeth II of England has officially opened the Royal website. Today she emailed a message to children attending a school in Canada.

Comment:
Nobody in Sandhaven Creek had plans to email the Queen, and this item of news went virtually unnoticed. Even by Ilma Mathews, who had her own symbol of royalty on her studio apartment floor.

A week later Rod was again on the highway, heading towards Tamworth. He approached the Dareboolah turn off and decided to find the gallery. He did not want to be looking for it in the dark later. He noticed the road he turned onto is Loxton Street.

He drove along Loxton Street, passing a sign which announced the township and gave its population as two hundred and sixty. He saw the gallery near the township centre. It was an old Mechanics Institute Hall, a solid brick building now carrying a wall sign beside the entrance. The sign read 'Vincent's Fine Art Gallery'. Rod laughed. Van Gogh may know something about art, he thought, but not our Vincent.

The gallery stood at the corner of Loxton Street and a narrower road called Parsons Street. He turned into the street to see if there was car access to the gallery grounds. At the gallery rear was a small new building extension and a garage. A short driveway between a gate and the garage offered too little space for overnight parking, but then, beyond the gallery and adjacent to its back boundary, Rod discovered an unfenced public car park with space for about twenty cars.

Just past the car park, Parsons Street ended at a T-junction. Rod took a left turn, which put him in the middle of a wider street called Grainger Road. There he found half a dozen shops and a few commercial buildings on one road side and a primary school on the other. A big sign on the footpath advertised a street market to be held on the fourth Sunday of every month.

"The city hub," Rod murmured to himself sarcastically. Satisfied he knew where to park later, he found his way back to Loxton Street and continued his journey to Tamworth.

★

Ilma was waiting for Rod. It was eleven twenty. He had phoned earlier to say he hoped to be there before then. She had set a coffee table with some plates, serviettes, a large platter of antipasto, a bowl filled with small bread rolls, an uncorked bottle of red wine, and two glasses. She had cleaned the en-suite, tidied away magazines, switched off the T.V., dimmed the lights, and three times attended to her hair. She looked around the room to see if anything else needed to be done.

It was a studio apartment of generous dimensions. On the side opposite to the entrance door was a small kitchenette recess, an ensuite, and a small walk-in wardrobe. The walls were white and decorated with a number of paintings and a full-length mirror. A single window and a sliding glass door, open onto a stone paved courtyard. Beside the window was the coffee table with the food and wine, and on each side stood a cane chair with a bright red cushion. On the other side, and used as a settee during daytime, was a three-quarter size bed, on which rest a number of similar cushions. A big red shag pile rug occupied the centre space.

Ilma wondered if she had time to go to the loo, and while she was deciding, the doorbell rings. She stood perfectly still for a moment, drew in her breath and let it out slowly. She moved to the door and opened it.

Rod entered quickly, looking a little flustered. "Been standing there under the porch light for everyone to see," he said, closing the door behind him. "Let's not have the light on again when you're expecting me."

Ilma was a bit deflated as she had not expected Rod's admonition. Realising he was right, she fingered off the offending light switch. She firmly put her arms around his neck and kissed him full on the lips. She clung to him for a while and then pushed him slowly away and, indicating the coffee table with a sweep of her arm, and said, "Wouldn't the Gypsy like first to eat?"

They sat at the coffee table. Ilma poured out two glasses of wine before shamelessly announcing, "I'm in urgent need of a pee. Make a start on the antipasto. I shan't be long." And she hurried off to the en-suite.

Rod sipped at his wine, taking in his surroundings. He thought it was quite classy. He leaned forward and put some pieces of cold meat, some cheese and a bread roll onto his plate. He was really hungry and his mouth was soon crammed full.

When Ilma returned she put on some music. She had been a Beatles fan ever since she first heard them. She selected John Lennon's 'Imagine' and turned the volume down low, so the music rhythm came through and did not overpower the lyrics. Her nerves relaxed with the music and she joined Rod at the table.

They sat there for a while, making small talk and eating. When nearly all the antipasto had been eaten and they had both consumed a couple of glasses of red wine, and after a pause in the conversation, Ilma looked at Rod and, waving towards the bed, she said quietly, "Shall we?"

She reached across and took hold of his hand and together they moved towards the bed. She nodded her head at the en-suite door and she asked, "Do you want to undress in there while I undress here, or," she smiled, "shall we undress each other?"

Rod did not answer in words. He just stepped up closer to her and started to undo the buttons of her jeans. When they were standing together, naked, he took hold of her shoulders and gently but firmly turned her around. He took hold of her wrists and put her arms straight down. Using only one hand, he pinned them together behind her back. With his free left hand he reached around her body and caressed her right breast, and with his mouth he nibbled the lobe of her right ear.

In exquisite bliss, Ilma realised this would be a truly exotic night.

7

Calm Before the Storm

Making news, Thursday 20 March 1997:
At a meeting today in Helsinki, Russia's President Boris Yeltsin and America's President Bill Clinton discussed expanding the NATO alliance to include countries of Eastern Europe.

Comment:
Whilst this may have be of some importance in the shaping of world affairs, Ilma Mathews was not in the least bit interested in the NATO alliance. She was busy plotting an alliance of a very different nature.

It was cold, dark and wet outside. Ilma awaited Rod's third visit to her apartment in Dareboolah. The studio room heater was full on and the curtains were drawn. The weather had been dreadful all day, heavy rain and frequent wind gusts. Nobody turned up at the gallery, and there were no artist appointments to be kept. Ilma had allowed Nadia to go home early, and spent the remaining gallery opening hours reading magazines.

At six o'clock Vincent made his usual Thursday night call to check if she was still at the gallery, and intending to stay over. She had told him she would be staying and he could safely depart for the club. She had devised a little white lie about an early morning meeting with a potential client. Well she had thought, with a wry grin, I am meeting Rod, and he does have potential.

On her way to the gallery in the morning, she had fortunately done some shopping in Dareboolah. Buying quite a lot of food and several bottles of wine, which she had intended to take home to Sandhaven Creek.

It was fortunate because at seven-thirty Rod had phoned to say the Greyhound meeting had been cancelled due to heavy rain, and he would be at the apartment at about nine-thirty. He said he hadn't eaten much, and so with plenty of food available, she had been able to offer him dinner. She was happy about this, for it meant she could set the right mood to present him with an idea.

Food and wine were not Ilma's only purchase for the day, she had bought something else which is bound to help. At the local haberdashery store she had found a pair of black silk lace knickers and a short black silk matching camisole. They were laid out on the bed ready to change into.

It would be at least another hour before Rod got there. She could allow herself the luxury of relaxing for a while. Careful not to crush the new underwear, she curled up on the bed and contemplated the possibilities over the next few hours.

Although her cooking skills were no more than adequate and the studio apartment's cooking facilities were no more than minimal, she had ambitiously decided to make gnocchi with bacon and mushroom in a cream sauce, and to follow this, a microwave heated rice pudding with a ready-to-serve egg custard. Everything was prepared and ready to cook, and she had some time left in which to think about her idea, and how to put it to Rod.

Their Thursday nights together had been so good, so enjoyable in many ways. But something was missing. Confinement to the apartment was restricting their affairs romance, which in her view, was now a love affair involving the heart, and not just a sexual adventure. Ilma felt lovers should have happy times together, apart from their bedtime activities.

They should have the pleasure of sharing each others company in a more romantic setting. And they need to be able to see and hear and touch, and speak to each other in an open flirtatious fashion, and proudly show to the world their happiness in being together.

All of which Ilma realised cannot be achieved if their only time together is spent in her small studio apartment at the gallery. Her desire to attain these other possible pleasures from her relationship with Rod, gave her the idea they could go away together for a few days. It would enable her to have the pleasure of his company, in a more romantic way. Somewhere they could dress up, go to a show, eat at a good restaurant, have a dance, and generally behave in a totally carefree way and in glamorous surroundings. And without the fear of being recognised.

Brisbane, yes, they would be free of prying eyes in Brisbane.

They could have a few days there together, she thought. But when should they go? Not at the weekend, it would be too dangerous for them both to be noticed as missing from tennis on the same day, and in any case, Rod would be too busy from Thursday through to Monday. But he could probably get away from Monday evening to Wednesday morning.

They would have to travel separately. Or at least start out as if. She could get the early morning Sandhaven Creek to Armidale coach, and fly to Brisbane from there. And Rod could drive up to Tamworth and get the late evening flight. And nobody would guess they were going to be in the same place together.

Then there was the matter of expenses. Rod, poor dear, probably hadn't even got the airfare, she thought. I expect the gallery account will have to cover it. Although Rod's ticket would have to be paid for in cash, or Brian would notice its purchase when he does the auditing.

A rumble of thunder interrupted Ilma's thoughts. She was never at ease during a thunderstorm, and she hoped it will soon end. The telephone rang and she gingerly picked it up. She believed it was not a good idea to hold onto the receiver while lightning was about. The caller was Vincent. He told her of a bad storm heading down from the north, wanting to know if she was alright. She let him know the storm had arrived, but assured him she is fine and reading a book.

As she hung up the phone she felt touched by Vincent's concern, but she was too focused on Rod's coming visit for her deception to trouble her. She was now living in two worlds, although the world of comfort and safety she had shared with Vincent was slowly shrinking. Yet it was part of her persona, and she was still dependent upon it.

Ilma knew she would have to add to her deception and tell Vincent another lie. And it would not be difficult to contrive one. She could tell him she had to make a business trip to Brisbane. He would buy the story, because she had made two previous visits of this nature, both in connection with gallery purchases and new display methods. Even if not happy about it, he wouldn't object. No, there won't be any problem with Vincent, she thought.

Satisfied she had sufficiently thought her idea through, Ilma turned her mind to the tactics required to persuade Rod into going away with her. She thought she should first drop a hint half way through dinner, then later, before making coffee, she would tell him she was going to put on something more comfortable. She would make sure he got a few opportunities to admire her in her new purchases. Then, over coffee, she could get down to seriously coaxing him into agreeing. Yes, this is the best approach, she thought. Oh, and she should mention early on the gallery can pay all costs, or Rod may hit the idea on the head before he even considers it.

Ilma glanced at her watch. It was nearly nine o'clock. Time to start the mushrooms cooking and to get changed, she thought.

As she rose to her feet there was another rumble of thunder. It was nearer this time, and much louder. She started the cooking the mushrooms, then walked back to the bed and softly ran her fingers over the silk of her new lingerie, before peeling off her clothes and putting on the seductive underwear, and re-dressing herself. From the bathroom she retrieved a white terry towel robe and laid it on the bed ready for later. She gathered up her old undies and shoved them into a holdall, and pushed it into a cupboard. As she entered the bathroom again, to tidy her hair, a massive clap of thunder immediately overhead sent her heart pounding with fright. God, it was close, she muttered aloud, and she felt herself trembling. She chided herself for her fear and went to see how the mushrooms were doing. All the lights go out suddenly, and her evening began to unravel.

Groping her way around, Ilma found a candle but had no means of lighting it. She kept a small torch in the gallery but remembered it was in need of a new battery, and in any case, she did not fancy going out into the storm to get it, or being in the gallery in the dark while she found it.

With the curtains drawn, the room was nearly pitch black. She parted the curtains, but it was such a dark night it barely made any difference. Several flashes of lightning gave momentary illumination, but added no value to her evening. All she could do was sit in a chair and wait for the storm to pass and the electricity to be restored. This proved to be a futile hope for a lightning bolt had hit a power pole transformer and there was no maintenance personnel stationed in the township of Dareboolah. It hadn't yet dawned on Ilma, but there would be no enticing dinner and no visually alluring lingerie display tonight.

Some time elapsed. It felt like an hour to Ilma but she had no means of knowing, she couldn't see the fingers on her watch and the normally illuminated bedside clock was electrically powered and had stopped. The last rumble of thunder, not very long ago, had come from a long way off. But the rain was still belting down in tropical fashion. She was beginning to worry about Rod. Suddenly, the sound of someone running and an urgent banging on the apartment door brought her to her feet.

Trying to get to the door quickly, Ilma knocked her knee on the coffee table edge and limped in pain for the next few paces. When she opened the door she could barely recognise Rod's figure, but there was no doubt in her mind he was soaked to the skin.

"Rod, thank heavens you are alright, come in, quick," says Ilma, flinging the door wide open, and feeling a blast of cold damp air penetrate the doorway space.

"What a bloody night," growled Rod, in a loud voice in order to be heard above the rain. He brushed past Ilma and came to a stop in the dark.

She closed the door. Her knee was still aching and the front of her dress was now thoroughly damp from the contact with Rod.

"Where is the light switch, I can't see a thing," Rod grumbled, as he entered.

"The electricity is off," she explained. "If you want to get your wet things off, just drop them on the floor. We can't do much with them until the power is back on."

"I still can't see a damn thing," Rod muttered, struggling to divest himself of most of his clothes. "I need a towel, Ilma. Can you find me one?"

Ilma saw the funny side of it and laughs. "If only I could see you, Gypsy. I'm sure you would look gorgeous." She grabbed his hand and led him to the bathroom, managing to do so without bumping into anything else. Fumbling about she found a clean towel and gave it to him. "Have you got a lighter or matches?"

"Look in my coat pocket. There should be a box of matches. They may be wet." Rod grunted, while vigorously towelling his hair dry.

Ilma found her way back to the fallen clothes and rummages about on the floor to find the relatively dry matches in his jacket pocket. She lit a candle.

In the flickering candle light shadows, Ilma moved around the apartment. She gathered up Rod's wet clothes, found a bottle of wine, and looked to see what was edible in the fridge.

"It's ruddy cold in here," Rod said, emerging from the bathroom. "Haven't you got a heater?"

Ilma was starting to feel cold herself. "The heater's electric," she said, getting close to him. Then putting her arms round him she added, "You will have to make do with body heat."

They stood together for a few moments, then Ilma broke away and pointed to her dressing gown. "See if it will fit you," she grinned.

Rod draped the robe over his shoulders, letting the sleeves hang loose. "What now?" He asked. "I saw a lot of damaged trees on the way here. I had got about half way when the storm struck, and there didn't seem much point in turning back, but I reckon it was easily the worst rain I have ever driven through. I doubt we will get the power back on tonight."

"Oh, Rod. It was going to be such a good night. I had

all this food cooking, and if the power doesn't come on again I can only give you bread and cheese."

Rod gave her a kiss. "Better than nothing, I guess," he said resignedly. And then in a brighter tone he added, "Looks like we will have to get warm in bed."

They had a few drinks and ate some bread and cheese, and then followed Rod's suggestion and cuddled up under the bed sheets.

After a period of energetic lovemaking, Rod was feeling peacefully drowsy, while Ilma was thinking of all the effort she had made in order to persuade Rod to comply with her desire to have a few days together in Brisbane. And the subject hadn't even been raised.

A lot of conniving, for nothing, she brooded.

Later, her mood changed. Maybe it is meant for us to be really living together? Yes, this is what I would really like, she thought. She put her lips close to Rod's face and whispered her thoughts into his ear.

8
The Lie

Making news, Saturday 5 April 1997:
An Irish Republican Army bomb threat has forced the annual Grand National steeplechase event at Aintree, near Liverpool, England, to be postponed.

Comment:
With its issue for Tuesday 31st December, the Sandhaven and District Journal had provided a free wall calendar, slipped between the centre pages of each delivered newspaper. The calendar recorded notable anniversaries, sporting, and other international events against the appropriate date indicators. Brian Clements had one of these calendars, and he read the notes on most days. Today however, thoughts of recent local happenings distracted him and, like most other people in town, he remained unaware the Grand National was due to be held, and was ignorant of its postponement.

Brian was in the kitchen on a Saturday morning, ready to go to tennis, and waiting for Jan to finish dressing. He idly looked at the wall calendar which Jan kept updated with reminder notes. He was a little surprised to see it had already been six weeks since Ilma's birthday party. He smiled to himself as he remembered Florian's drunken attempt to kiss Sally, and how Sally had Martial Arts'ed him and he fell on his back onto the settee. He had first looked startled and then put on a weak smile, and fallen asleep. Vincent had later effortlessly lifted him off the settee and carried him into a bedroom and laid him on a bed, where he had stayed until, at three o'clock in the morning, Jan had declared she would not go to bed while Florian was in the house. She and Brian woke him up and got him into a taxi.

Brian thought Florian was almost certainly an alcoholic. Whenever Brian saw him after midday, he was always shushing his words and swaying on his feet. Brian assumed he did his painting in the early morning periods, while he could still hold a paintbrush. He wondered what the work in Florian's forthcoming exhibition would be like. Jan had marked the opening day on the calendar, and added 'six-thirty ceremony'. Well well, mused Brian, no way would Florian remain standing for the speech.

Brian heard Jan call out she was ready. He left the kitchen and went to meet her at the front door. As soon as he stepped outside the house, Brian noticed their car had a flat tyre. When they eventually got to the tennis courts they were nearly half an hour late.

They saw Rod and Sally and a couple of new members playing on Court One. Four older teenage members were having a hit up on Court Two, and Vincent and Ilma were sitting on a bench beside Court Three. As they approached the courts, Vincent called out. "We were just thinking of ringing you two, come and join us here."

Together all four went onto Court Three and without

any discussion they paired off at the net, Vincent and Jan to one side, and Brian and Ilma to the other. Vincent, despite his large frame, was not as good a player as Brian, and they knew from experience they would have a better game if Jan played with Vincent, as her height gives her an advantage at the net over the much shorter Ilma. They enjoyed playing until they reached one set all, then honour satisfied, they retired to the pavilion for afternoon tea.

Rod, Sally and the new couple were already sitting at a long table, sipping coffee and nibbling biscuits. Ilma casually walked over to them and pulled out one of several spare seats at their table. The others follow suit. Nobody noticed Ilma's deliberate selection of chair. A chair favourably positioned to enable her to see Rod clearly without appearing to be too close to him.

Sally motioned to the new couple and made the introductions, identifying the newcomers as Tom and Toni. "Pour yourselves some coffee and have one of these," she said, pushing forward a plate of chocolate biscuits. "And what kept you, Brian?"

Brian made up four coffees, and then told them about the flat tyre. He passed the coffee around and then turned to Toni and asked, "How long have you two been living in Sandhaven Creek? I don't think I've seen either of you about the town."

"No," replied Toni. "We've only been here a few weeks. We moved down from Armidale. Tom is with the Department of Agriculture. He's working out at the dam until June, and then the Department is opening a district office here in Sandhaven Creek, and Tom will be its Manager. I'm teaching at the high school."

"Oh. And what do you teach?"

"I teach art to the senior students in years ten to twelve. You haven't seen much of me because the school hasn't had an art teacher for over twelve months, and consequentially I've had a lot of extra preparation work to do. Just about caught up now, thank goodness."

Brian stirred his coffee and asked, "Do you do much painting yourself, Toni?" Then, trying to draw Toni into the group rather than just having her reply to his question, he slightly raised his voice and added, "Ilma has an interest in art, don't you Ilma?"

Ilma, sitting a few chairs away, seemed reluctant to enter the conversation, which surprised Brian, but eventually she muttered, "I have a gallery. It's out of town. I mostly exhibit artists from Tamworth and Armidale, and I get a few works from Melbourne and Brisbane artists."

Brian had expected Ilma to open up more, and to encourage Toni to answer his question. He was a bit surprised when she didn't and for a moment there was silence. Then Ilma spoke again, and with more enthusiasm in her voice. "I'm sorry Toni," she said. "I didn't mean to be rude, my mind was elsewhere. Brian was asking if you are doing any painting?"

Toni said, "Oh, well actually I do try to paint regularly, mostly in watercolours. But it has been difficult to find time recently. I have exhibited but I've nothing in my studio at the moment. I must come and see your gallery though, Ilma."

Rod heard her and moved the conversation in a

different direction. Looking at Toni he said, "I'm the local rag reporter. We run a 'welcome to new citizens' column in the Journal. You could take pity on me and let me do an article on you, maybe including a photo of you demonstrating to the students. I'm sure the school wouldn't mind. It'll be good publicity for them."

Rod and Toni chatted away, discussing a possible scenario for the article. Jan, Sally, and Vincent were talking to Tom about the S.C. and Brian and Ilma sat listening.

Brian was still pondering over Ilma's earlier lapse in manners when he became aware of something else. He noticed Ilma was not paying much attention to the conversation about the club because she was continually switching her gaze towards Rod and Toni. He remembered he had seen a certain look on her face as she had glanced at Rod at the barbecue in Possum Park, and he saw something of the same in the way she was looking at Rod now. He tried to see if Vincent had noticed but couldn't see Vincent's face as he was leaning away from him, emphasising to Tom the S.C. bistro's virtues.

Brian was an observant man, but he tried to see the best side of people. He remained silent. He and Ilma had been friends for a long time and he had never considered her as being flirtatious. But a little seed of doubt about this was now sown in his mind. And he didn't really want to believe it.

★

Making news, Monday 7 April 1997:
The Brazilian Government today adopted legislation to criminalise torture, and through this legislation has established a Human Rights Secretariat to monitor police conduct. The Pulitzer Prize awards winners are to be announced in New York City today.

Comment:
Both news items failed to register interest within the Sandhaven Creek community, wherein police force members were inclined to be helpful rather than hurtful, while intellectual writers preferred to live elsewhere.

On Monday morning, Brian had to talk with Mrs. Vorcer. She was a domineering woman who was the Sandhaven Ladies Guild Chairperson, a fundraising organisation which supports various charities. It was a torrid meeting which lasted for over an hour.

After she left, Brian felt like his brain had been scrambled. He glanced at a few notes he had made and clipped them into a file relating to the Guild's business. He decided he needed some fresh air and he went through to the reception area where Maureen was working. "If you haven't picked up the mail yet," he said to Maureen, "I'm looking for an excuse to clear my head after dealing with the Chairperson from Hell."

Maureen smiled. "She's a bit of a dragon, isn't she? And no, I haven't picked up the mail." She turned to a cupboard behind her, took a key off a hook inside it and tossed it to him. Brian slipped it into his pocket and set out for the Post Office.

He turned left on leaving his office and walked a short distance to a pedestrian crossing. He then continued his walk on the other side of Main Street, strolling along at a leisurely pace until he reached the Post Office building which stood on the corner of Harvey Street.

The building was of Colonial style, with a colonnaded walkway along the two street frontages. The walkway provided covered access to the Post Office entrance off Harvey Street, and to the mailboxes and locked private letterboxes, which were set into the wall facing Main Street.

As Brian approached the building he saw Ilma standing close to the walkway corner. She had her back to him and appeared to be having an intense low-voiced discussion, with someone who was just out of sight around the building corner. He could tell from her body language, she was all fired up.

Brian collected his mail and took another glance towards Ilma. She was shaking her head and pointing, as if indicating something further down Main Street. She raised her voice and almost shouted, "I can't help it." Then she walked quickly away in the direction she had pointed.

Thoughtfully, Brian turned and walks towards his office. He stopped at the newsagency a few doors away from the Post Office. He entered the shop, picked up a copy of the 'Financial Times', and took it to the counter. As he paid for it he saw Rod walking past the shop doorway, and he wondered if it was Rod who had been talking to Ilma.

He returned to his office and carried on working. He had a sandwich lunch at his desk and then continued with his tasks. At four fifteen the phone rang. He answered it and heard Vincent's voice. "Brian, how are you? I just got home, and I found Ilma a bit down in the dumps. She's complaining she hasn't been able to leave the house all day. You know how it is. Well, I thought it'd be a good idea if we went out to dinner tonight. I'm thinking the pub may be bit of a change for her. And I wondered if you and Jan could be interested in joining us?"

"It could be. I'll let you know. If I ring now I may still catch Jan at the shop." Brian put down the phone. Well, well, he mused to himself thoughtfully. What is going on?

Either Ilma considered her morning Post Office visit not really 'leaving the house', or she didn't want Vincent to know she went to town this morning. It did look like she was arguing with someone, and I reckon it was probably Rod, thought Brian. It dawned on him that something was going on between them, but of what nature? Surely Rod wasn't trying it on with Ilma? He wouldn't be so daft, Vincent would put him in hospital if he found out. Maybe he was getting it all wrong and it was something quite innocent. Could it be Ilma was planning some kind of surprise for Vincent? Was it something to do with The Journal perhaps?

He picked up the phone again and dials Jan's number. They discussed Vincent's invitation, but he didn't tell her about seeing Ilma at the Post Office. He would have been bombarded with questions.

9
Sally's Secret

Making news, Monday 7 April 1997:
The black pearls, which represent ninety percent of French Polynesia's export revenue, today recorded a 46% sales increase over the last year.

Comment:
Sally Tully had bought some black pearls in Paris some years ago. She viewed them as an investment and hardly ever wore them. She kept them in a bank safety box, and every year she checked their likely value. The next time she checked their worth, she was very surprised indeed.

At the barbecue in Possum Park a few weeks earlier, Sally had mentioned she liked men to be nearer her own age. The truth was she had always been attracted to men who were several years older than herself. It was always highly probable Sally would one day fall in love with a married man, and this she did. She fell in love with Vincent. It happened shortly after their first meeting. However, Sally, being Sally and very loyal to her friends, had never mentioned this to anyone, least of all to Vincent.

Five years before, Sally had arrived in Sandhaven Creek to take up a position in the Town Planning Office. On her first lunch break in her new job, she went into the local supermarket and found herself standing next to Jan. It took them a few moments to recognise each other, and then they realised they had stayed for a few weeks in the same hostel in Europe, and had gone shopping together one day. They got on very well at the time but later went in different directions.

On renewing their acquaintance when they met at the supermarket, Jan invited Sally home to dinner, and a very firm friendship developed between them.

When Sally had been in Sandhaven Creek for about a month, Jan introduced her to Ilma and Vincent, and encouraged her to join the tennis club. From then on Sally shared many hours of pleasure in the company of her new friends. However, about three months after joining the tennis club, something happened. Something Sally will forever remember.

It occurred at the tennis club on a Saturday afternoon. Brian had been unable to play because he had a client to see, and Ilma and Jan had been asked to play in a ladies double set, so Sally found herself sitting alone with Vincent while they waited for a vacant court. She was happy to be sitting with Vincent, for she admired him greatly. And from time to time in the past few months she had covertly watched him, noting his strong physique and healthy colouring. She had begun to recognise some of his mannerisms and to anticipate his reactions to certain events or conversation trends. And what she saw as a mix in his general character intrigued her. She thought he was intelligent, knowledgeable, and a leader amongst men, yet there was about him a sort of boyish naivety, which she liked.

They were sitting very close together and their arms touched. It was at this moment she came to understand the true meaning of happiness, and realise she had fallen in love.

This realisation came as a shock to Sally. She had never ever considered the possibility of falling in love with a married man. She had always thought love happened mutually between two people, but only if they are free to make romantic advances to each other. There have been no romantic exchanges between she and Vincent, and absolutely nothing to indicate any mutual feeling on Vincent's behalf. She had never intended to make any physical contact with him, nor could she have foreseen its effect would be so unequivocal.

It was not her fault, it was all about chemistry. She was in love with Vincent, and he was married.

The problem for Sally was what to do about it. There had been no reaction from Vincent and she was well aware of Vincent's devotion to his wife, and she believed her chances of changing this situation would be next to zero. But she also instinctively knew her love for Vincent would be timeless, and she would never be able to give herself to any other man. After much soul searching, she decided it would be pointless for her to give up her job and try to re-start her life away from Vincent. If I cannot keep him out of my mind, she thought, I might as well keep him in sight.

The ensuing years had been hard for Sally, for she was not naturally a frigid woman. Many men had been attracted to her, but none had ever shared her bed. She had kept her love pure and secret, and tried to console her heart as she restricted herself to only being with Vincent, when he was in the company of his friends. Doing whatever little things she could which she knew pleased him, little things which would not give away the secret of her affection for him. Wanting so much to be with him every day, but restraining herself from ever again being with him alone. And all the time believing, given different circumstances, she and Vincent would unite as one.

Sally was a kind and gentle soul – intelligent and practical. Nevertheless, she sometimes fantasised about Vincent's marriage to Ilma breaking up. In these fantasies she visualised dreadful things such as Ilma's death in an accident, or Ilma falling out of a boat and drowning, or even her having a heart attack or committing suicide. Immediately after each fantasy Sally would tell herself she didn't really want any of those things to happen to anyone, let alone her friend. She did, however, allow herself to hope Vincent and Ilma's marriage would one day come to an end through less harmful causes.

It was not surprising Sally had stopped to look out of her office window earlier today.

The Town Planning Office, in which Sally worked, was located on the Town Hall building second floor, and the window near her desk overlooks the Post Office Square. So she too had seen Ilma talking to someone in the Post Office cloisters, but unlike Brian, Sally did not have to guess who was with Ilma for she could quite plainly recognise it was Rod. And Sally had been able to see, before Ilma's body language indicated a disagreement, she had been standing very close to Rod and was clutching his arm.

It was only for a few moments Rod and Ilma had been together, and then Sally saw them part. Rod going towards the letterboxes and Ilma, obviously agitated, walking very quickly towards the Town Hall. Afraid Ilma may look up and see her, Sally moved away from her window. Sally could hardly believe it, but what she had seen looked more intimate than just a tiff between two friends, and Sally felt a little thrill of excitement at the thought of Vincent and Ilma's relationship being more insecure than she had supposed. But Sally resolved not to make too much from the scene she had just witnessed. She would be too disappointed if she was wrong.

10
Bets & Beats

Making news, Thursday 1 May 1997:
From a platform of brining about sweeping changes, Tony Blair leads the British Labour Party to victory and was today appointed Prime Minister of the United Kingdom.

Comment:
This may have been a momentous occasion for Tony Blair, but for Rod Skapleson, the day was to be remembered for other reasons. Brian Clements discussed the matter with his wife, saying Tony Blair seemed almost 'too good to be true'.

Rod eased his foot off the accelerator as he traversed a long bend in the road, some ten kilometres north of Sandhaven Creek. He thought about his night with Ilma the previous Thursday. How she had been waiting for him, having on only a light dressing gown, barely closed at the front. And how she had invited him to do whatever he liked with her when they got into bed. And how, just as he was going off to sleep she had spoilt it all. She had started another conversation about the possibility of their going away to live together somewhere, and had more or less forced him to agree to think about it.

His thoughts wandered on and, in his mind, he pictured

her at tennis in her short dress with halter top. He smiled and reached forward to turn on some music. Then, on a darker note, he thought of how she had kept trying to catch his eye at tennis, and how, fearful Vincent may notice, he had studiously avoided her attentions.

Which, of course, was why they had an awful argument at the Post Office, when he had attempted to tell her how risky it was for her to be carrying on in such a way in Vincent's presence, and yes, he had thought about what she had said in regard to going away together but he needed more time to think about it. He had told her there were practical things to consider like, what they would do for money, where to live, where to get another job, and whether to sell his car. Well he had no intention of selling his car, but he had to tell her something, didn't he? He was not quite ready to give up the joys of her bed just yet. Well, why should he? She had understood at the outset, it was intended to be nothing more than a romantic adventure.

The car caught up with a large truck, and he had to wait for a clear road ahead before he could overtake it. He concentrated on his driving, until he passed the truck. The road cleared and he seized the opportunity, pushing the accelerator down hard, surging around the truck, and quickly returning to the correct road side. Then with the truck a good hundred metres behind him, he continued his thoughts about Ilma.

He had seen another side to Ilma when, at the Post Office, he had attempted to chastise her for taking unnecessary risks at the tennis club. She did not want to hear about it. She had said Vincent wasn't ever going to notice, and she could not help how she felt and if she wanted to look at him she would, no matter who was there. He realised it was getting dangerous for them to be together amongst friends, because Ilma's feelings towards him were blinding her to the need for caution. He wondered how Joe Bernaldo may react if he found out his favourite reporter was having it off with the wife of one of Sandhaven Creek's most respected citizens. "Shit," he said, under his breath.

"One of Sandhaven Creek's respected citizens," he muttered, turning his mind to Vincent and doing a brain talk to himself. Well, now I've got to know him better, I can see why. He's a nice guy, and this is a problem, he thought. When I started this fling with Ilma I didn't know him so well. Wouldn't have let it happen if I had. Been a lot of help to me has our Vincent. Fixed my door and made a good job of it and I appreciate his help, even though I could have done it myself. And he did make it easy for me when I got my S.C, membership through. Showed me around and gave me a good wrap up in an introductory speech. And then there was the incident a few nights ago when a drunken guy picked on me, and Vincent quickly stepped in and sorted him out, despite the guys near giant size. Yep, I have to admit Vincent is a nice guy, a sort of softy with a firm hand. Maybe I should break it off with Ilma pretty soon. Well, say after enjoying a few more nights with her.

But as he passed the Dareboolah turn off he knew, that when the time came to break it off with Ilma, she would resist the idea fiercely. So with an uneasy mind he drove on toward Tamworth.

★

In Tamworth, Rod went through his now usual routine of visiting the agency, dropping off his overnight bag in his Bridge Street room and hiding the cheque book and envelopes under the bedside cabinet, ringing Ilma, having a quick meal, and then heading to the race track.

At the track on this particular day he was on his way up to the commentary box when he bumped into Chuffy Tornton. Chuffy put a hand on Rod's chest and said, "Hold on a minute, Rod, I've got something for you." He lowered his voice and continued, "I know you don't usually have a bet, but tonight there's a horse in Race Five which I tell you cannot be beaten. Watch out for 'Glowing', John Prendergast trains it over in Armidale. My sister-in-law's cousin owns him. He bought the horse in Melbourne as a three year old, gave it a couple of races with an inexperienced driver and, from dreadful runs, it finished third both times."

Chuffy looked around conspiratorially. He rubbed his finger against his nose, and he winked at Rod, "Well," he almost whispered, "It's like this. He realised the horse is something special and he decided to hide it away for a year, and to put punters off the scent, he gave it a start in a handicap at Graverton Park and made sure it only finished fifth. Should start at about five or six to one, but if you get in before the stable money goes on you may get as high as twelve, I tell you Rod, this is a proper tip. Put a few dollars on Glowing, and you won't regret it."

Rod thanked him and continued on his way to the

commentary box, which he shared with Ted Braxton. Ted had the race running sheets spread out on the bench before him. He looked up as Rod entered.

"G'day, Rod," he said. "I've finished the scratching list, there's a copy for you on the bench. I see we've a couple of new trainers here tonight, Reggie Manderson and Tony Van-Ewing."

"Oh, what are their colours, do you know?"

"Yes. Tony Van-Ewing's driver is wearing yellow with blue bands on the arms and a yellow and blue quartered cap. One of his horses is favourite in Race Six, and he has another horse in Race Four. The word is he's an experienced trainer who's moving his stable down here from Brisbane. We'll probably see a lot more of him in the future."

"And, Reggie Manderson?"

"Manderson is totally new to the game. He got his licence last week. Used to be a boxer, then had a couple of greyhounds. He is known around the town as a bit of a no hope type. He'll be wearing pink with white spots and a white cap."

"I take it he's driving himself?"

"Yes, he only has one horse. Race Two. Could be a winner, it's well backed on the tote."

"Do you know anything about a horse called 'Glowing' in Race Five? Chuffy stopped me downstairs. He said it's a good thing."

Ted looks at the race guide. "One of John Prendergast's horses," he said. "Got Errol Wiseman driving it. They could be a useful combination. It's a bit unusual for Chuffy to be giving out tips, he knows the game alright but he usually sticks to managing the canteen. Mmm, I might have a few dollars on it myself. You never know."

Rod changed the subject and asks, "Can you do the last race for me tonight, Ted? Something special on and I would like to get away early."

"Sure, Rod. Not a problem. I'll ring you the result in the morning. What time will you get back to the Journal?"

Rod hesitated for a moment before saying, "Not sure really. I've something to do in Tamworth in the morning, perhaps eleven thirty. If I'm not at the hotel number, talk to Joe Bernaldo. I'll be ringing him first thing in the morning. If all else fails, I'll ring you, okay?"

They proceeded with their evenings work, alternating between them the tasks of describing the warm-up parades and the actual race calls, and both taking notes for the next day's news reports. Rod kept thinking about the tip Chuffy has given him and decided he could afford to lose $40. As soon as the all clear for race four sounded, he went down to the betting ring and over to the tote window. He knew enough about racing to realise he would be recognised in the bookies ring. They might pull the odds down before Ted can get a bet on, he thought. However, when he got to the tote window he realised he would only get the starting odds if he placed his bet there, and, if the stable money went on the tote, this could easily drop to as low as five to one. So he forgot about Ted and went to the betting ring. He was right, there were quite a few people who recognised him, but his conscience about Ted was quickly soothed when he saw most bookies were offering

Glowing at fourteen to one.

He returned to the commentary box and told Ted what he had done. Ted said he would risk $10 and quickly left the commentary box. Ten minutes later he was back and said, "I could only get eleven to one. There's a bit of money going on for Glowing. Maybe it's got a chance."

They kept their eyes on the tote dividend board and saw Glowing's odds drop to nine, then to seven, then to six and finally down to five to one. "Looks like Chuffy's come up with the goods," said Ted.

Chuffy had indeed come up with the goods. Glowing was a two lengths winner, and Rod was $560 richer.

★

One race later, as soon as its results had become official, Rod gathered up all the information he had collected during the evening and put the notes, race sheets and newspaper clippings into his briefcase. He thanked Ted for letting him get away early, and he left the commentary box. As he descended the commentary box stairs, he felt pleased with himself and looked forward to spending the night with Ilma.

When he got to ground level he walked over to the betting ring to collect the winnings from his bet on Glowing. Greg Newton, the bookies clerk, took his betting slip. "Ouch," he said, "another bloody Glowing punter." He counted out $600 and handed it to Rod.

Frank Foley, the bookie, looked at Rod, and with a dark face said, "Don't you load any more of your money on to me lad, it won't be welcome. You guys up in the box must think we're dumb. Well I know from the betting, a tip must have gone out, and I also know who the regular punters are, and who aren't. And you ain't one of em, so I know you have a contact 'cause you took this bet at fourteen to one, before anyone had even heard of the bloody horse. Well okay, I accepted the bet, but don't be so bloody greedy next time. Put your money on the tote and leave us bookies to make an honest living from the mug punters."

Rod was not so sure he agreed with Frank's idea of an honest living, but he didn't not want to make any enemies on the premises. He could see Frank was real mad so he pushed the money into his pocket and said, "I get your point, always willing to take advice, Frank, guess I owe you one." He departed from the betting ring as quickly as he could without drawing too much attention to himself. But he was not quite quick enough. A couple of doubtful looking young layabouts, one wearing a red beanie hat, had been probing around hoping to find thrown away winning tote tickets. They were searching the ground near enough to Frank's bookies stand to overhear his tirade and they realised this smallish well-dressed man with a briefcase is a punter who had won more than a couple of dollars.

Rod was still feeling pleased as he walked down the exit pathway. He had $600 in his pocket and a vision of Ilma awaiting him in her sexy, not quite fully covering, dressing gown. "Nice night," he said to the gatekeeper as he passed through and heads towards the car park.

Quite a few people were leaving before the last race started. A number of expectant taxis were waiting just outside the gates, where there was plenty of overhead lighting. An enterprising salesman with a sausage sizzle cart, was doing well off successful punters. Rod thought he would like a sausage but the allure of Ilma is too much, so he quickly crossed the well-lit area and walked into the car park darker recesses.

Rod found his car and decided to transfer the money from his pocket to his briefcase. He did not want to risk having Ilma see it. If she saw the money she would only push him harder with talk about them going away together.

He put his keys and the briefcase on the car bonnet, opened the briefcase and took the money out of his pocket. And suddenly, his world fell apart. He received a mighty thump on the back of his head and another thump in the small of his back, just above the left kidney. His knees buckled and he felt himself fall to the ground. There was a loud cracking noise as his face made hard contact with the wing mirror on the car. He was on his back and, as if in a mist, he could see four legs. Then the kicking began and all consciousness was lost.

Perception returned to Rod slowly, first the pain, which seemed to be all over him, then the vision, showing him to be lying between two cars, and then full comprehension. "The bastards," he muttered, and found himself spitting out blood.

His keys, the briefcase, and the money were gone. He felt inside his jacket pocket to find he still had his wallet.

A young couple had seen what happened and were running towards him. The guy was pretty big and out of breath. He had chased after the layabout with the beanie hat, but wasn't fast enough to catch him. Their car was parked only two spaces from Rod's, and they insist on taking Rod to the hospital.

While waiting for attention he rings Ilma from the nurse station desk. "Hi. It's me. A bit of a problem I'm afraid. I got mugged at the races. I won't be with you for supper, they took my keys as well as my money. I'm at the hospital to get a stitch in a cut lip. It'll be okay. Can't talk now, I'll be getting attended to in a minute and then I have to make a police report. The couple who brought me here saw the whole thing. Look, I have to go, I'll phone you in the morning."

"Oh Gypsy, I'll come over and see you. You can come back to the flat with me."

"I don't think you should come to the hospital. You know why."

"Yes, I suppose it would be risky but I was so looking forward to tonight, I'm not sure I can wait another week. Maybe you'll be better in the morning. Give me a ring, and if you're feeling frisky we may still get together here for a while. Nardia won't be here to open the gallery until midday. You are alright, aren't you?"

"Yes. Sorry love. I'll phone you as soon as I can tomorrow. Must hang up, the doctor's coming." Rod ended the conversation because he really didn't feel up to it. He just wanted to get his lip fixed, the police report done, and to get back to his room to sleep.

He knew, however, there was one small problem yet to be solved. How to get into his room? He would have to ring Beryl. He looked at his watch and noted it is eleven fifteen. Beryl would probably be in bed because she gets up at six thirty. With a sigh he dialed Beryl's number, which he fortunately could remember because it only contained fives and eights. A sleepy voice answered.

"Hello. Beryl Thomas speaking, who is this?"

"Beryl, it's me, Rod Skapleson."

Rod paused, wondering how Beryl would react. Beryl interjected, the sleepiness in her voice replaced with surprise. "Rod, Rod, what is it, where are you, are you in your room?"

"No. No Beryl, I'm sorry to bother you so late but I've had an accident. I'm at the hospital. I'm alright and as soon as I can get checked out I'll be getting a taxi back to my room. The trouble is I've lost my keys and I won't be able to get into my room. Can you leave me a spare key somewhere, or perhaps unlock my door for me? Sorry I've had to wake you, Beryl, but I didn't know what else to do. I sort of don't fancy sleeping in the yard all night."

"It's okay, I'm awake now. How bad was the accident, Rod? Is your car a write-off?"

"Oh, it wasn't a car smash. No. I was mugged at the races in the car park. They stole some money and my car keys. They stuck the boots in and I've a few cuts and bruises, nothing serious, it is not life threatening."

"Do they want you to see a doctor?"

"Yes."

"Have you seen one yet?"

"No. I'm waiting in the emergency room."

"Well look, Rod. Now I'm awake I know I won't be able to get to sleep again. It is just me, if I wake up I have to get up and have a cuppa or do something physical, or I never get back to sleep. So forget the taxi. I'll drive over and get you."

"You don't have to, Beryl. A taxi will be fine."

"Oh yes I do. I'll be there in say thirty minutes. Now don't argue."

"Mmm, alright, I won't argue."

A nurse called his name and asked him to follow her to a screened examination bench. He explained to her what had happened and asked if she could make a police report. He saw the doctor, got a couple of stitches in his lip wound, had a grazed patch on his forehead cleaned and dressed, was thoroughly examined, and then sent off for x-ray to check for any bone damage to his skull.

When he came back from the x-ray room, Beryl was waiting for him. A policeman was asking at the desk where he could find the race mugging victim. When Rod had given the policeman all the necessary details, the x-ray results were ready. He had to see the doctor again, but the doctor didn't return for another half hour.

At twelve forty-five Rod was told the x-rays showed his skull to be alright and, providing he took things very quietly for the next forty-eight hours, he could go home.

Beryl drove him to the hotel. She told him his room was not booked out to anyone else until Sunday and if he wished he could stay there till then, adding, it would be on the house with meals included. Rod was in no condition to argue so he gratefully accepted. Within twenty minutes he was in bed and closed his eyes.

★

Making news, Friday 2 May 1997:
Following the President's last-minute decree yesterday, the Cameroon's citizens will today celebrate a Public Holiday.

Comment:
Rod Skapleson had a day off.

Rod awoke at nine o'clock in the morning. His joints were stiff and his body was aching all over. His mind cleared and he remembered what happened the night before, and considered all of its implications. He had to get in touch with Joe Bernaldo, and he must phone Ilma. Then he had to find out where his car was and how to get a new key, and he had to see Beryl. He told himself he must make the call to Ilma his first priority. There was no way he would be able to get to the gallery before midday, and he didn't want Ilma to come looking for him at Bridge Street.

With a bit of a moan he suppressed the desire to remain still and forced himself to get out of bed. He wrapped a blanket around himself, sat down on the bed edge and picked up the phone. It was not a direct line system, so he dialed '0' for reception. Beryl answered.

"Oh. Hi, Rod. How are you this morning, plenty of aches and pains I'll bet?"

"Moaning and groaning a bit, but I am on my feet. Thanks for all you did for me last night. I really do appreciate it, Beryl. I'd like to repay you some way, maybe take you for a meal, say next week, when I'm in better condition."

"This sounds good. How is your mouth? Can you eat breakfast? Perhaps something soft, like cereal with sliced bananas and seedless grapes, some orange juice, and a coffee. Be ready for you in the dining room in half an hour, okay? I might have a coffee-break with you, and we can discuss where you're going to take me as penance."

"Yes, of course, but could it be in forty-five minutes though? I need to take a long hot shower and then make some phone calls. One is particularly urgent. Can you give me a line, I had better get on with it. Thanks again Beryl, see you shortly."

He rang Ilma. "Sorry love. I just woke up."

"How are you? I missed you terribly. My bed felt quite empty and I couldn't get to sleep for ages. Are you coming over?"

"No. I'm too sore I'm afraid. The doctor said I have to take it easy for a couple of days, so I'm staying in Bridge Street. The hotel is letting me have the room until Saturday morning."

"Oh, my poor Gypsy. I wish I could kiss you better. If you like I can come and see you."

"I wish you could, love. But the proprietor here is a friend of Bebe Eisler's, our local agent. And Bebe talks a lot to Joe Bernaldo, and Bebe knows who you are. So I think it's too risky, and anyway, I don't want to get too excited, I need to rest up today. Look, I'm sure I'll be fit enough to visit you next Thursday."

"But I miss you Rod. I'd just like to be able to see you before then. Why don't you come to have afternoon tea at tennis, and I'll try to make an excuse to sit out a set so we can talk. At least we'll be able to see each other. I promise to be very discreet."

"Well, okay. I miss you too but we'll have to be very careful. I'll get there if I can but I cannot guarantee it. It depends on how Joe might be coping without me today, and whether he needs me tomorrow. And right now I have to phone Joe, he doesn't know anything about this yet, so it's urgent I ring him. Sorry love, got to go, as they say. Be careful driving home. Love you."

"Love you too, Gypsy."

Rod quickly hung up. A couple of harmless little lies in that conversation, he thought, before picking up the phone again to call Joe. He explained his situation to Joe and told him Ted Braxton will be ringing the Journal with the race results. He assured him the advertising copy was safe and that he would get it on Saturday morning. He also told Joe he would be writing an article on his own mugging, and he asked Joe to keep some front-page space available.

Next, he phoned Ted. And then the racecourse Manager, who told him his car was safe and standing in Munro's Towing Services yard.

Rod decided to have a shower and to defer any more phone calls until the afternoon. After the shower he felt much better and had no problem in getting himself dressed and walking over to the dining room. As promised, the table was laid and breakfast was ready.

Later, Beryl took away Rod's empty breakfast plate and returned with two black coffees. She looked at his stitched lip and smiled. "Perhaps I should put milk in your coffee to cool it down, or," and her smile broke into a laugh, "If you like I can fetch you a straw."

Rod sat there, feeling surprisingly relaxed. Nobody had mothered him since he was just a little kid, and he appreciated Beryl's efforts to comfort him. He refused the straw offer but accepted the milk suggestion and managed to sip slowly away at the coffee. He and Beryl engaged in some pleasant conversation and, for the first time in his life, Rod found himself talking with a woman on equal terms.

As his confidence grew, Rod told Beryl he had trouble in the past in forming proper relationships with women. He explained how, before arriving in Sandhaven Creek, nearly all the women he had been acquainted in his short adult life, he had met in pubs or at public dance halls. He explained that he found them mostly to be hard, uncaring, not too intelligent, and only interested in themselves. He admitted to Beryl he had, until recently, developed an irreverent attitude towards women. But his new job had enabled him to meet women like Sally and Jan and Contessa, and he was only just beginning to see women in a different light.

He talked about Sally and Jan and Contessa, and how clever and well informed he thought they are. And he confessed he was almost in awe of them, and how sometimes he had to disguise his inferiority feelings when in their presence.

Beryl's sympathetic ear emboldened Rod, and he gave out more information about himself. But much as he was enjoying this new experience of candid discussion, he had not yet acquired the courage to tell Beryl about his separation from Norma, nor of his affair with Ilma. In both of these matters he was still very much aware that secrecy was vital.

11
Concern

Making news, Friday 2 May 1997:
In Washington DC, a monument has been dedicated to former United States President Franklin D. Roosevelt. Roosevelt played a significant role in bringing about the Nazi forces defeat in World War II, and spent much of his life in a wheelchair following an attack of poliomyelitis in 1921.

Comment:
By remarkable coincidence, a man named Rolly Roosevelt was Mayor of Sandhaven Creek during the last two years of World War II. He died in 1980 and it was later discovered he had fraudulently embezzled a large sum of money from the Building Society of which he was manager. His grandson attended Vincent Mathews' school, and his conduct had caused Vincent to request a meeting with his parents on a number of occasions.

The day after Rod's mugging, Vincent was at school working on routine tasks, which included staff reports, notes on re-programming to cover the loss of a teacher for two months, several letters from parents, school requisitions, Education Department memorandums, advertising material, and P. & T. meeting notes.

When Vincent finished, it was well after school hours. There had been quite a distressing incident late in the afternoon when separated parents had turned up at the school, each claiming the right to take their little girl home. The mother had become quite shrill in her attempts to convince him she was the one, and the father, nearly in tears and clutching the child to him, had to be physically restrained from taking the child. It turned out the mother had the child's legal custody, but the little girl had been with the father for nearly three weeks while the mother was away on holiday, and the mother had returned two days earlier than expected. The matter was eventually resolved, but not before Vincent and one of his staff had insisted upon taking the child into Vincent's office while the parents sorted it out in an empty classroom.

So when Vincent walked into his house at six fifteen he was feeling mentally zapped, and looking forward to a quiet drink with Ilma before heading off to the club. He went through to the lounge and found Ilma sitting in an easy chair with a partly filled glass of wine in her hand.

She raised her glass to him. "You're late tonight," she said, draining the glass in one gulp and then pouring another.

Vincent mentally noted Ilma had not followed her usual practice of putting a glass out ready for him, and he wondered if it is just forgetfulness on her part or whether something had happened to upset her. She didn't usually worry if he came home late, she knew long hours came with the job. He gave her a kiss, but he didn't get the expected arms around his neck response, and he realised she was sitting in an easy chair and not on the sofa, where they usually sit together.

Vincent got a glass from a drinks cabinet, poured himself a sherry, and sat on the sofa. "So what has happened in your day?" he asked. "You don't seem terribly happy."

Ilma thawed a little. She had been fretting all day, trying to get over not seeing Rod for a whole week, and she was having difficulty trying to keep up the pretence with Vincent. But she knew this is necessary and it was churlish to be cross with him.

"Oh, sorry Vince," she said, trying hard to be composed. "It's not you. I'm just down in the dumps. Nothing has been sold at the gallery this week. And when I got home I cleaned out the laundry. Then I decided to go through some cupboards in the bedroom. I finished up sorting out some clothes to give to the Salvo's, and now I'm tired, and I don't want to go to the club tonight. I'm afraid you'll have to go on your own."

Vincent was thoughtful. He could see something is wrong. Ilma usually took any kind of physical work in her stride. Lack of energy had never been a problem for her, and he had often marveled at what she could get through in a day, but Vincent was mentally exhausted after his torrid day, and he didn't want to press the issue at the moment. He sat, swirling the wine in his glass.

Shortly, and just as a matter of conversation, he asked, "What time did you get home?"

"About one o'clock, I think. I left the gallery at midday. And what happened to you? What kept you so late?"

Vincent told her about the parents who were separated and the trouble they had caused. Ilma said, "Oh," and took another sip of her sherry. Vincent noticed her lack of interest in the conversation so they sat in silence for three or four minutes before Vincent got to his feet. "Well, I have to go," he said quietly. "I have to call the bingo tonight. Maybe you should have an early night love, huh?"

When he got to the S.C. club, Vincent had made up his mind Ilma was not her usual self, and hadn't been for several days. He thought she was getting tired too easily and maybe she was not well.

★

Making news, Saturday 3 May:
The 123ʳᵈ annual Kentucky Derby was won today in a photo finish by Silver Charm, ridden by jockey Garry Steve.

Comment:
The Sandhaven Creek Horse Racing Club's only event was a once a year 'Picnic Day' race meeting, which coincided with the famous Melbourne Cup race held in Victoria. Rod Skapleson had been to a Melbourne Cup race but had not yet attended a local Picnic Day meeting. On this day, he told of his more recent racing trouble at the meeting in Tamworth, and wondered if anyone had had a similar experience at the Kentucky Derby meeting.

While preparing for tennis on Saturday, Vincent again became worried about Ilma's health. She had told him she still felt tired after yesterday's house cleaning, and may only play two or three sets instead of their usual four. Vincent suggested they come home early, but she quickly assured him it will not be necessary and she would be quite happy for him to stay and play the extra sets.

Vincent watched her as she changed into her tennis dress. Stripped down to her bra and panties, Ilma looked anything but sick. Her smooth tanned skin and trim waistline gave out an impression of peak bodily fitness. Standing on her left leg as she put on her right sock, she balanced with the ease of a trained ballet dancer, and in wriggling into her tight fitting short tennis dress, she showed off an agility usually associated only with a person of healthy physique.

Because Ilma showed no outward signs of illness, as he believed she would if she had the flu or any other common virus related sickness, Vincent became even more worried. He was aware there were diseases, such as cancer, which do not affect the bodily image for some time, and he started to dwell on the possibility of Ilma having contracted something of this nature. He felt he couldn't talk to her about such a distressing conception, but he made a mental note to persuade her to go for a general medical check-up if her tiredness continued.

Vincent did not like the idea of Ilma becoming seriously ill. There was so much pain and suffering attached to it, and oh, the ever present danger of never recovering. To see Ilma, his beautiful wife and good companion, transposed into a frail, pain wracked invalid with yellowed skin and haunted eyes, would be quite devastating. He doubted he could bear it and tried to dismiss all thought of it from his mind.

He picked up one of his tennis shoes to find the laces had knotted. The concentration required to undo the knot was a blessing. He had little success in undoing the knot and his frustration began to show. Ilma saw his problem and opened a dressing table drawer. "I bought a few spares," she said, offering him a pack of new white laces.

The moment of worry passed.

The act of reaching for his tennis shirt put he and Ilma close enough together for him to feel the heat of her body. How come, he thought, I only seem to get randy at the wrong time?

Later at tennis they played two sets against Sally and another club member called Bob. Afterwards they all headed towards the pavilion. It was a lovely sunny day, with the temperature in the low twenties. On the way, Ilma suggested they sit outside for afternoon tea. "If we put enough chairs out, the other players will just join us," she said.

Vincent agreed, and while Ilma and Sally busied themselves in the pavilion kitchen, he and Bob carried a number of director-style folding chairs out, and placed them on the lawn. They finished this task as Jan and Brian and a number of other players came off the courts.

Ilma and Sally brought out afternoon tea and Ilma organised things so Vincent's little group of close friends could all sit together. Vincent went off to the toilets. When he returned, Rod had arrived and was sitting with the group. Vincent saw Rod is not dressed for tennis and was looking a bit worse for wear.

Rod told them about his mugging, and about Chuffy

Thornton and his tip. He illustrated how he fell against the car wing mirror and showed some of his bruises. While he was talking, Ilma handed out coffee and Sally served up cakes. When he has finished his story, Rod reached for another cake. "These cakes are terrific," he said, "who made them?"

Sally answers, "Jan made them. They're her speciality. Quite yummy aren't they?"

Rod nodded and looks at Jan, "You can bake me a cake any time, Jan," he proclaimed. "These are even better than my mum used to make."

Jan smiled, she was obviously flattered. She offered to bring him some next week, just for himself, to take home. They all chatted for a while, then Sally announced she was ready to play another set. Ilma, in full view of everyone, went up to Vincent and lightly touches his arm. "You won't mind if I sit this one out, will you Vince?" she asked. Then without waiting for an answer, and looking towards Sally, she added, "You can take Sally as a partner, and Brian can play with Jan for a change. I feel I need a bit of a rest after two straight sets, Bob sure plays a hard game. Casually she walks over to Rod and leading the way to the pavilion, she calls back, "Come on Rod, you can help me wash the dishes, and I'll play in the next set."

It was all done smoothly and naturally, as if she was politely hinting to a new member about everyone having to muck in.

As soon as they were alone in the pavilion, Ilma pointed to a kitchen corner which couldn't be seen through the partition windows. "Let's go over there," she said, pushing Rod in the general direction.

When they reached the corner Ilma put her arms around Rod's neck and kissed him full on the lips. "I need some caressing," she murmured, rubbing her breasts against his chest. "But don't get me too excited, will you?"

"If you rub against me like this it'll be me who gets excited."

"Ooo, that would be unkind of me, wouldn't it? I don't want you to become a frustrated lover." She gave him another kiss then broke away. "I'm so glad to be alone with you for a while." She paused and put on a worried expression. "Oh," she continued, "I'm sorry, I forgot about your lip. Does it hurt when I kiss you?"

"No. It's fine now."

"Good. I'll give you another kiss, and then, we must do the dishes."

★

Vincent, having been pre-warned Ilma may not feel up to playing four sets, walked towards the courts in company with Sally. He confided to her Ilma is not quite herself at the moment, and he feared she may be sickening for something. Sally's heart beat faster. She suspected the only thing wrong with Ilma was infatuation, but she didn't want to tell this to Vincent. She preferred to let it run its course.

12
Jan the Spy

Making news, Friday 9 May 1997:
The new United States Ambassador to Vietnam, Douglas Peterson, arrived in Hanoi today. He is the first person to hold this post since the end of the Vietnam War.

Comment:
The Sandhaven Creek Citizen's Social Club was originally a Returned Servicemen's League Club established during World War II, and with an influx of Vietnam War Veterans it survived as such until 1990. However shortly after this, a decline in all War Veterans numbers forced it to open its membership to civilians. In the following year it expanded the club premises and changed its name to reflect its current objectives. A private meeting room was provided for the remaining Veterans.

Friday night, a week later, Jan and Brian were starting their second cup of coffee when Vincent joined them in the S.C. bistro. It was eight thirty and Vincent had just finished his duties at the bingo session, calling the numbers and presenting the prizes. Jan thought he looked tired and he is not his usual hearty self. She and Brian were also wondering if something had happened to Ilma. She had phoned them earlier to say she and Vincent were having a quick meal at home and would not be joining them for dinner, but Vincent would be doing his M.C. stuff as usual and would join them for coffee later. Ilma had said she herself would be having an early night, because she had a busy day coming up tomorrow.

Brian poured Vincent a glass of red wine, then volunteered to go and buy him a coffee.

Jan looked at Vincent, "You look bushed, Vince," she said. "It must be quite exhausting calling out all those bingo numbers and all the sayings, like 'clickety-click' and 'Kelly's eye'. I don't know how you can remember them all."

"Oh, I suppose it's just become a habit. And if I do forget, well, I just ad lib. Like instead of calling 'number four, knock on the door', I might say, 'number four, get off the floor'. It's all a bit silly really but it's what the players pay their money for. So how has your day been, Jan?"

"Not bad. I got a lot of customers at the shop today, it about doubled the normal Friday take. I was run off my feet for a while but it's surprising how much energy one can find if business is doing well."

They were quiet for a moment. Jan nervously fingered the stem of her wine glass. "Talking of energy," she continued her voice low and hesitant. "I must confess my conscience is troubling me. How is Ilma? Last week after tennis you said you thought she might have been sickening for something."

"When Ilma phoned me earlier to say you wouldn't be here for dinner, I had a pan of soup on the stove getting it ready for lunch tomorrow. It started to burn and I had to rescue the pan, and I didn't have time to ask Ilma how she was. Nothing serious developing, I hope?"

"No, I don't think so. She gets tired and a little bit irritable, which isn't the real Ilma, as you know. But she says there's nothing wrong with her, and she doesn't need to see a doctor. I must admit though, Jan, I'm a little bit worried about her. She seems sort of listless lately, as if she isn't at all interested in things. Doesn't want to sit and watch telly and doesn't want to go out much either."

Jan was touched at Vincent's concern, but she thought if Ilma was not seeing a doctor then she probably didn't have much the matter with her. Ilma took good care of herself and was proud of her body. If she had the least sign of something wrong, she would be off to the doctor in a flash.

Jan suspected there might be a more interesting reason for Ilma's apparent listlessness when in Vincent's presence, but her suspicions were not well enough founded to broach the subject, and she wondered how she would act if they were. However, she could see Vincent was worried and wanted to talk, so she said, "Maybe Ilma is a little bit depressed, do you think?"

"She could be. I sometimes wonder if she's disappointed we don't have any children. One of those things, I guess. And maybe it is starting to worry Ilma, but she doesn't talk about it."

"I'm sure not having children is not the problem, Vince. You know, we girls get together and we talk about these things, and Ilma has never mentioned to me any deep yearning to be a mother. In fact, rather the opposite, she has expressed several times the opinion she's glad she isn't tied down like some of our friends. So I wouldn't worry about this aspect, it's more likely she's just going through a stage in her life and may be temporarily depressed. Just be kind to her, Vince, and wait and see."

"Yes. You're probably right, Jan. I guess if there's anything really wrong she'll eventually tell me." Vince paused for a sip at his wine, then continued with a change of subject. "Now, about tomorrow. Our new terrace is ready and I'm having a barbecue to celebrate. Ilma suggested we invite you and Brian, and perhaps Sally and Rod. We can ask them at tennis tomorrow."

"Oh, lovely, what do we bring?"

"You can bring absolutely nothing."

Brian arrived with Vincent's coffee. Vincent picked up the cup and in a grateful tone continued, "Thanks Brian, I can murder a coffee. We're talking about a barbecue at our place tomorrow night, and Jan has volunteered your presence."

★

Making news, Saturday 10 May 1997:
A severe earthquake in the north-eastern region of Iran has killed over one thousand five hundred people.

Comment:
Vincent heard this news on his radio as he prepared for a barbeque party at his home. The news saddened him and he commented on it to his guests when they arrived.

In the morning, while Brian was putting in a couple of hours at the office, Jan was busy in the kitchen doing some baking. Jan was quick and deft with her fingers, and it wasn't long before she had turned a number of ingredients into a couple of dozen ready to bake Eccles cakes. She placed the cakes onto a baking tray and put the tray into the oven. She set the oven timer, and cleaned up the kitchen.

Jan looked at the clock and saw it was nearly an hour since Brian left. She didn't expect him back for another half hour, which was just about the time the cakes will be ready. She opened the kitchen window, so she would hear the timer, and then went out into the garden to do some weeding.

Several buckets of weeds later, the oven timer noise brought her back into the kitchen. She went over to the oven, looked at the cakes and decided to give them another ten minutes to brown up on top. As she closed the oven door she heard Brian enter the house, calling out, "Hi dear. What's cooking? Smells great."

He approached Jan and gave her a kiss, then opened a cupboard and took out a bottle of sherry and two glasses. "I think it is time for a drink?" He say's.

Jan laughed. "Always," she replied, emphatically.

"What have you been making?"

"I've been making some more Eccles cakes to take to tennis. And before you ask why, I do know it's actually Ilma's turn to take afternoon tea, but these cakes are only for Rod. He liked the ones I made last week so much, so filled with flattery, I promised I would make some for him to take home."

Brian wrinkled his nose, "I thought it was a familiar smell. Save a couple for me, will you? You don't want me to get jealous of Rod, do you?"

"No need for you to be jealous, dear. But I do think Ilma finds him attractive. I've seen her giving him a look a few times."

"So have I," said Brian while pouring out two drinks. "In fact, I feel a bit guilty because I've been wondering if Ilma is getting to be a little flirtatious."

"I don't think so, I haven't seen her making eyes at anyone else. I do hope she doesn't allow Rod's charms to fool her. I reckon he's the type who could easily lead a girl into deep water, if he wanted to."

"What type is that then?" Brian asked, passing over a glass.

"The small, dark, handsome, type; with come to bed eyes."

"Oh, so you've noticed, have you?" Remarked Brian, mockingly.

"Yes. I picked him out as soon as I met him. But I can see him for what he is."

"I thought you liked Rod?"

"Yes dear, I do. But I wouldn't trust him with my little sister, if I had one."

"So you think Ilma is in danger?"

"Yes, I think I do."

"I hope you're wrong. I'd hate to see Vincent's reaction if he found another guy with Ilma."

The phone rang. Sally was on the line to say her tennis racquet had a broken string. She asked if Jan or Brian had a spare racquet she could borrow.

Jan assured her she had a spare and would bring it with her. Then Sally asked if Jan would like to see a film next week, and they talked for a further ten minutes. Jan put down the phone only to find Brian had walked off into the lounge with his drink. And the topic of Ilma's flirtatiousness was forgotten.

★

It was three o'clock in the afternoon when an unexpected heavy shower of rain drove all the tennis players into the pavilion. Jan looked around and couldn't see Rod anywhere amongst them. She asked a few people if they had seen him but it soon became apparent to her he had not turned up to tennis. She saw Ilma making coffee and went to join her.

"I was expecting to see Rod here," she remarked.

Ilma was silent for a moment, then said, "I expect he's busy," and changed the subject. "Has Vincent spoken to you about the barbecue tonight?" she asked, "I hope you and Brian are coming, Vince did a lot of shopping this morning, and our fridge is full to bursting."

"Yes," replied Jan. "He told us all about the barbecue last night. I can see Vincent over there talking to Sally now, so I expect he'll be inviting her. He said he'd also invite Rod but I guess Rod's bombed out, since he isn't here," she paused, then added, "unless Vincent has already spoken to him?"

"No, he hasn't," snapped Ilma. "And it's too late now unless he turns up for afternoon tea as he did last week."

"I hope he does." Jan nodded at a basket she had just

put on a table. "I brought him some cakes. If he doesn't come I'll have to take them to him later. I cooked them especially for him to take home. He said he liked them so much."

Ilma gave her an odd look. "I'd better get on with afternoon teas," she said. "I've only brought chocolate biscuits. Not all of us can cook."

The players continued their afternoon tea. The rain shower had stopped, but it produced enough rain to form puddles all over the courts, and the players generally agreed to abandon any further play for the day. A couple of junior players had a different view and went out onto the least affected court and tried to mop it dry using sponges and buckets. All the other players sat around and chatted for a while and then went home. Jan and Ilma, for different reasons, both delayed their departure in the hope Rod might make a late appearance, but it was not to be.

★

At Vincent's barbecue, Jan and Brian were introduced to Vincent's new next-door neighbours, Carol and Andy Davies. The four of them get into healthy discussion before Sally arrived to join them.

"Carol," said Jan. "This is a friend of mine, Sally Tully. Sally, meet Carol and Andy. They have just moved in next-door."

Everyone chatted for a while before Ilma loudly announced, "Grub up. Plates and cutlery are on the side table. Vince is about to serve up the meat, so come and sit down and help yourselves."

Brian took Carol's arm and, in no time at all, they were all sitting around a large garden table. Spread over a white cloth are platters of barbecued meats and sausages, and bowls of cooked mushrooms, fried onion rings, French fries, and salads, together with bottles of beer and red and white wine, and a large basket of bread rolls made from a variety of wheats. Vincent had really turned it on, thought Jan.

At nine o'clock, while Vincent was in the kitchen getting a bottle of soft drink for Anne, the phone rang. It was Nardia De Cloose, Ilma's gallery Manager. Vincent took a cordless receiver out to Ilma and told her Nardia wanted to speak to her. Ilma rolled her eyes but didn't get up from the table, and when she spoke into the phone, everyone at the table could overhear her part of the conversation.

"Hello, Nardia, anything wrong?

Oh, I see. Well, I guess you have to.

Yes, okay, we don't need to open on Tuesday.

What? Oh damn. No, don't you worry, I'll do it.

What time is he coming?

Nine sounds fine. What is he interested in?

Did you say Magnus Opstein's 'Country Bride' portrait? Hmmm. What do you think he'll pay?

Oh! You've told him more than I was thinking we could get. Well then, he must be interested. It might make my trip worthwhile.

Don't worry. Yes, I know. I'll stay all day. Look after your mum Nardia."

Ilma terminated the call, put the receiver down, and

caught Vincent's eye. She directed her voice to him. "Nardia's aunt has died and her mum is upset. Nardia's leaving for Toowoomba first thing in the morning."

Ilma paused, looks at Vince, and then continued. "I'm sorry, Vince. Apparently we have a Brisbane buyer who is staying in Tamworth and he has an appointment to see one of our better pieces at nine o'clock in the morning. And it's market day so I'll have to keep the gallery open all day."

Jan could tell Vincent was not at all pleased but she saw him nod and say to Ilma, "Yes, okay. I had nothing special in mind for tomorrow. I'll get a bit of gardening done. It might be a good chance to repair the section of fence over near the shed."

Carol asked Ilma about her gallery, what sort of paintings she exhibits and where it was located. Andy honed in on Brian and told him he needed some professional advice. Sally and Ilma spoke about food, and Vincent and Jan discussed a local planning issue.

Subjects changed and people moved places. The conversation ebbed and flowed until, at about eleven thirty, Jan declared herself ready for bed.

★

Making news, Sunday 11 May 1997:
Deep Blue, the chess-playing computer developed by scientists and chess experts, has won against Garry Kasperov. The world champion conceded the fifth and final game after the 19th move, thus losing the match with a score at three games to two.

Comment:
Brian Clements was unaware of this news, but his own latent interest in chess was re-awakening.

Jan was out of bed surprisingly early on Sunday morning, despite her late night at the barbecue. After cleaning her teeth she woke Brian up, an hour before his usual nine thirty Sunday morning getting up time.

"Come on, sleepy head. If we're going to Dareboolah market you had better get out of bed before the sun goes down."

Jan bent over and gave him a kiss, then sat on the bed beside him. "On the way, do you mind if we see if Rod's at home? I want to give him the cakes. I've a really busy week coming up and if I don't take them today I may not get another chance till next weekend. And even Rod probably wouldn't eat them then. By the way, what do you think of Rod? It's very hard to get anything out of him, don't you think? I mean, the other day he even avoided telling me where he was born."

"Yes, I do find him a bit secretive. But, you know the Sandhaven Creek motto, 'ask no questions and you get no lies'. He seems okay. Sally likes him and she's usually a good judge of character. And he is a good sport, doesn't sulk if he loses and he doesn't skite when he wins. And his general knowledge is quite good. All the same, I do have some reservations, but I can't put my finger on why."

"Mmm, I feel a bit the same. But right now, Mr. Brian Clements," she laughed, vigorously pulling off the bedclothes. "You're either going to find me on top of you or you're going to get up."

"Huh. Why the alternatives, can't you get on top of me for a while, and then I can get up?"

"Oh. You. Come on. Get out of bed, there's always tomorrow." Jan got up, throwing him a dressing gown. "You can shower with me if you like," she said, with a big grin.

After breakfast they set out for Dareboolah, via Possum Park. At the park they found there to be no one in the caravan. A neighbouring van owner explained Rod had not been there since Saturday morning. Jan asked him if she could leave a box of cakes for Rod for when he returns, suggesting to him he should eat the cakes himself if Rod did not return by tomorrow. They were a bit puzzled at Rod's absence and discussed possible reasons for it as they continued their trip to Dareboolah.

They arrived in Dareboolah at a quarter past eleven. Vincent's Fine Art Gallery had opened its doors to the public, and Brian was able to park outside its entrance door. The sky was clouding over and the temperature had dropped, so Jan put on a lightweight jacket as soon as she ventured from the car. They entered the gallery to find it was empty of people except for Ilma, who was sitting behind an eight foot long table which serves as a desk. Ilma was sitting at the desk looking at a magazine, drinking a large cup of coffee.

"Oh, this is a nice surprise," she said. "What brings you two slumming on a Sunday morning?"

"Curiosity, I suppose," replied Jan, with a smile. "We're here to buy some homemade marmalade and some mushrooms at the market, and we thought we'd drop in and see what's new here since our last visit a couple of months ago."

"Oh, I've had two exhibitions on since then, but now we're back to some old favourites, most of which you've probably seen." Ilma paused. Raising to her feet she asked, "Have you time for a coffee?"

Brian looked at Jan then said, "No thanks, Ilma. I think there's rain on its way. We'll have a quick look around, say a few appropriate oohs and aahs, and get on our way to the market before the clouds get lower."

Ilma nodded. "I know," she says. "It does look threatening. I listened to the local forecast on the way here. The prediction is for heavy rain between two and three o'clock, but those dark clouds indicate it could come sooner. I washed my car on Friday, well, I took it through the car wash, so I've put it in the garage just in case. Hopefully, the rain will clear before I'm ready to leave."

Brian wandered around, looking at paintings. Jan stopped to concentrate on a small display of hand-made jewellery, made from local materials. Eventually Brian came to a blank patch on a wall. A small printed card indicated it was recently filled with Magnus Opstein's 'Country Bride' portrait. The price was $3000. "You sold it?" he said, questioningly.

Ilma nodded her head, "Yes, he left with it about twenty minutes ago. There was no haggling over the price, so Magnus will be pleased. And so am I, it makes sitting here all day almost worthwhile."

Jan went over to look at a display of miniature watercolours and saw one which she thought will look very nice on the wall near their telephone. It was an affordable $75 so she decided to buy it.

On their way out they passed another couple who were just entering.

★

Brian moved the car around the corner and into Parsons Street. There was no space left in the corner car park and the market stalls occupied the whole of Grainger Road between Parsons Street and the Goodgee Street roundabout, so he couldn't turn left. Instead he turned right and then left into Church Road and found a space in a larger car park behind the Grainger Road shops.

They left the car and walked through an arcade where they almost bumped into Rod Skapleson. He was accompanied by Beryl Thomas.

Rod was obviously surprised to see them, his face flushed with embarrassment, but for them all the meeting was too sudden to enable avoiding acknowledgements. So they stopped to talk.

Jan could see Beryl, although youthful in appearance, was actually a good deal older than Rod, and she wondered what their relationship might be. She gave them a pleasant smile, "Why, Rod," she said. "We missed you last night. Vincent put on a great barbecue after we finished tennis. Oh, and we went looking for you earlier this morning. I've left some cakes for you with your neighbour."

Rod looked a bit nonplussed, and then it dawned on him. "Aah, the Eccles cakes, great," he said, and quickly added, "Oh, let me introduce you. This is my Tamworth landlady, Beryl Thomas. Beryl, this is a couple of my Sandhaven Creek tennis mates, Jan and Brian Clements."

Jan looked at Beryl. She thought Beryl seems to be a nice friendly sort of person and she warmed to her straight away. She smiled and said, "Nice to meet you, Beryl. We're here to buy Ma Dawson's homemade marmalade. It's absolutely fabulous."

Beryl's eyes twinkled. "Oh, I know it only too well. I'm here for the same reason. I buy it in bulk, two cases of it every third market day. This is why Rod is here, to help me carry it. He's doing penance," she laughs. "He can tell you why."

Rod laughed too. He seemed to have got over his earlier nerves. "I'm saving the cost of an expensive dinner," he said, then goes on to tell Jan and Brian how Beryl had helped him the night he was mugged. And how he had offered to take her to the exclusive Tamworth Hilton for dinner, but she had talked him into helping her at the market and having lunch instead. "And this is what she calls my penance," he concluded.

From Rod's explanation, it dawned on Jan that Rod was embarrassed to be seen with Beryl, not because she was his girlfriend, but rather, because she was not. Now why would this be, wondered Jan.

They all walked together, pausing at various stalls as they made their way towards Ma Dawson's stall. Jan purchased three jars of marmalade and put them into a string bag, which she had with her. Beryl paid for her own order, two cases containing a dozen jars each. Ma Dawson, whose real name is Ruth Nicadopolous, points to a trolley. "There it is, love, all ready for yer. Yer will bring the trolley back soon, won't yer? 'Course yer will, luv. Yer won't want me to get caught wivout me trolley when the rain comes, will yer. 'Ave a good day, love."

Rod collected the trolley. It was a small two wheel carriers trolley that was easy to push. Beryl put a restraining hand on his arm and said, "Can we go to the next stall before we take these to the car? There is something I want you all to see."

She guided them over to it, and Jan laughed in delight, "What cute little things," she said, looking down at a cage of baby Angora rabbits. She realised the whole stand was filled with cages of rabbits of different shapes and sizes. "Are these here every market day? I don't think I've seen them before."

"No," said Beryl. "He has a shop in Tamworth, it's set back a bit from the road, and if the weather is right he often has the stall out on the pavement. I recognised it as soon as I saw it. I thought you'd like to see them, pretty little things, aren't they?"

They all turned to go back, and found themselves face to face with Carol and Andy Davies. Jan introduced them to Rod and Beryl and told Rod they are Vincent's new neighbours.

Rod was disturbed. He could see how easy it was for news to get around, and in particular, to get to Vincent's ears. If he and Ilma were to be seen together, even in Dareboolah, the chances were Vincent would soon hear of it. Carol and Andy held another danger for him, the possibility of Ilma learning of his visit to the market with Beryl, and not knowing who Beryl is. Rod's life was suddenly getting complicated.

Carol told them they had been at the market since ten thirty and had already made one trip back to their car with a bag full of goodies. She went on to say they intended to call at the art gallery and see Ilma, and thank her for last night's barbecue. They then excused themselves, saying they must be on their way to their daughter's before two thirty,

Rod was looking a bit uncomfortable. As soon as the Davies were out of earshot, he addressed Jan. "Did they say they're going to visit Ilma?"

"Yes. But of course, you wouldn't know. You weren't there last night. Ilma has an art gallery here in Dareboolah, just round the corner in Loxton Street."

"Oh, I've heard about it, but I thought she had someone manage it. I didn't know she works there herself," said the flustered Rod, untruthfully.

"Only on special occasions," Jan informed him, and went on to tell Rod about the phone call Ilma received at the barbecue. Then she turned to Beryl. "Are you interested in art, Beryl?" she asked. "Ilma has some nice pieces in her gallery."

Before Beryl could reply, Rod quickly interrupted. "I think we'd better get these boxes back to the car. I booked a table for lunch at Jo Jo's Bistro in Tamworth and by the time we've returned this trolley it'll be just about time to head there."

Beryl smiled. "The final part of his penance," she said, "I let him off the more expensive dinner promise. Very pleased to have met you both, and we must watch out for each other, Jan, next time we're stocking up on marmalade." They both laughed and they all shook hands except for Rod, who was already two steps away and picking up pace.

★

Making news, Monday 12 May 1997:
Russian President Boris Yeltsin, and Chechnya President Aslan Maskhadov, have signed an agreement to stop violence between their states. The agreement falls short of resolving the real issue of Chechnya becoming fully independent of Russia.

Comment:
The uncertain situation revived memories of Cold War days of the KGB, of spies in foreign embassies, and of veiled and sinister political threats. This was unlikely to cause much concern in Sandhaven Creek, but one of its residents showed some interest in spying on somebody.

On Monday morning, Jan was working. She was the proud

Proprietor of Quinky's Coffee Shop in Harvey Street, just around the corner from the Sandhaven Creek Post Office. At about ten thirty, she gathered up some accounts and slipped them into a file and picked up an account book. Armed with the file and the book, she stepped out from behind the counter and looked back at her young assistant, Lorraine. "I'm taking these over to Brian," she said. "I'll only be about half an hour, back in time for the lunch rush."

Leaving the shop she walked to the corner of Harvey Street, then turned left into Main Street. At the roundabout she crossed the road and continued walking down Main Street towards Brian's office. She saw Ilma come out of Pullman Street, and walking ahead of her on the opposite pavement. Ilma was striding along looking to neither right nor left, and showing none of her usual interest in shop window gazing. Jan was a little bit amused at the sexy swing of Ilma's hips, something she had not noticed in her friend before.

About ten seconds before reaching Brian's office, Jan saw Ilma enter The Journal building. Brian's office and The Journal building are almost directly opposite to each other, and given her longer legged advantage, she was surprised she hadn't caught Ilma up.

Jan opened the door to Brian's office and went over to his desk.

"Hi lover," she said. "I've brought the accounts over." She walked around his desk and leaned over to give him a big kiss.

A slightly embarrassed receptionist, Maureen, followed

her in to the office and offered Jan coffee.

"No thanks, Maureen. I'm only staying for a few moments, just long enough for Brian to tell me he now has all he needs to audit my books," she said, handing the books to Brian and moving towards the window.

Maureen departed, closing the door. Brian glanced through the files Jan had given him, and then leafed quickly through the accounts book. "Yes," he said, "this is all I need, everything else is in the computer. What's the rush?"

"Oh, there is no rush, I do have a few moments, but I've just had a coffee at the shop. Oh, I'm sorry, did I stop you from getting one?"

"No. I've had one. Are you going to sit down?"

Jan laughed. "I can see better standing near the window."

"What are you looking at?"

"Well, nothing at the moment. I saw Ilma going into The Journal offices, she was looking very determined. I'm just curious as to why."

"Sounds a bit like spying to me?" Brian said, raising his eyebrows.

Jan glanced quickly at him, before returning her gaze to the window.

"Yes, but it's fun," she said mischievously. "And here she comes and she has Rod with her. They're getting into his car and she looks furious. You don't think they're having an affair, do you?"

"It's possible, but I hope not. This is a tittle-tattle town' We have both seen her giving him looks. But let's not jump to conclusions. From what you say she doesn't seem to be keen on him at the moment."

"Well, I think it's all very odd. What other reason would she have for seeing Rod? And why would he be interested in Ilma, she's ten years older than him?"

"Some men do like an older women, it gives them a sense of security."

"Do you think he sees Ilma as a Linus blanket?" laughed Jan.

Jan stood in silence for a while then said, "They're getting from the car. Ilma seems a bit happier, she's holding onto Rod's arm. Rod is saying something to her and she's nodding her head. Rod is leaving her now and going back into The Journal's offices. Ilma is walking off towards Pullman Street. Now she's stopped to look in the Nicholl's Boutique window. Oh bother, she's going inside."

"Well, thank you for the running commentary, and what does the master spy deduce from all this? And anyway, what do you mean, oh bother?"

"What I think is they've had some sort of misunderstanding and it looked like they were having a lover's tiff. And 'oh bother' means I have a guilty conscience and I don't want to bump into Ilma until I've sorted it out. And now I'll have to wait here until she leaves the shop and goes on her way."

Jan continued to stand near the window, keeping an eye out for Ilma. Suddenly she said, "Brian, what do you think Vincent would do if he thought Ilma was having an affair?"

"He would probably kill the guy, and then go and buy Ilma a present to get over it. I doubt if he would openly blame Ilma because he still wouldn't want to hurt her, but he would be very cut up inside."

"Poor Vincent, she doesn't know how lucky she is to have him. I know how lucky I am to have you. Oh good, she's coming out now. I'll be able to go soon. I do hope we're wrong about her."

"Well, I suppose we'll know one day."

Jan came away from the window. "I will never ever deceive you Dear," she said quietly, and gave him another kiss before leaving.

13
Florian Gets Drunk

Making news, Thursday 15 May 1997:
Theo Weigel, the German Finance Minister, has proposed a revolution of the country's currency reserves in order to support public finances and conform to European economic and monetary union plans. The proposal is not popular with the majority of his countrymen.

Comment:
Ilma Mathews shrewdly and secretively assessed her own financial position and wishfully concluded it to be adequate for her planned objective to succeed.

In her Dareboolah apartment behind the gallery, Ilma looked at the calendar. It showed it was Thursday the 28th of March. Ten weeks since Rod first slept here, she realised, as she idly picked up a magazine then put it down again. She mixed herself a gin and tonic and sat in a red cushioned cane chair, moving it slightly to get a better view into the courtyard. It was nine thirty in the evening and not yet dark. She was restless, but forced herself to try and think clearly. She was certain she was in love with Rod, but she couldn't be sure Rod was as deeply affected as her. She recognised she would have to believe he was in love with her to some degree, and she must do everything she could to nurture whatever love he did feel for her.

She thought she must live with Rod or lose her sanity. The incident at the weekend had shown her how jealous she could become at the thought of Rod with another woman. When Carol Davies had come into the gallery and told her she had just met Brian and Jan at the market, and had been introduced to a young reporter called Rod and his friend, Beryl, she found herself trembling with anger. She had been hard pressed to keep a smile on her face until Anne and her husband had left the gallery. And she had given Vincent a bad time when she got home. If she went on like this he would know she was having an affair. And of course, she dare not bail up Rod in his office again as she had done on Monday morning. It would be like telling the whole world something is going on between them.

She went on Monday morning – she just could not contain herself. She had to know who Beryl was and why she was with Rod at the market. And she had to know if she was the reason he had not been at tennis on Saturday. It was such a relief when Rod explained the situation to her. He explained how Beryl had declined his offer to take her out for a thank you dinner and asked him to help her out on market day instead. He thought Beryl had meant a market in Tamworth and was quite surprised when she drove him to Dareboolah. On Saturday night he had slept in his room at Bridge Street, he explained, because he had been all day in Tamworth covering the Tamworth and Armidale District Athletics meeting, and while Beryl was serving breakfast on Sunday morning, she had reminded him it was market day.

Now another problem loomed. On Tuesday night Vincent had told her he was worried about her health. He said he thought she was listless and lacking in energy. He had questioned her on the subject, and had suggested she should see a doctor. She had hated having to lie to him, but of course there was nothing wrong with her, and she certainly did not want to talk to a doctor. Nor did she want to go anywhere near a surgery waiting room, the hottest of all hotbeds of gossip, in her mind. So she had told Vincent she was just going through a busy period at both the library and the gallery, and he shouldn't worry so much.

Vincent had produced a number of holiday brochures, and presented them to her. He pointed out they contained some very good Bed and Breakfast places in which they could relax. He suggested we could stay at one over the long Easter break in a couple of week's time. He had asked her of she would like to select one, and he would go to the travel agent on Saturday morning and put a deposit on the booking.

The idea completely threw her, she appreciated the thought behindVincent's offer, but under the circumstances she felt she couldn't accompany Vince to a place of such romantic nature. Continuing to live with him at home was sufficiently deceitful.

She knew she had to end this deceit soon. She couldn't bear it much longer. To give herself breathing space, she was forced to tell Vincent it would depend on whether

Nardia can look after the gallery in the holiday period, and to give her a chance to think about it, they may have to wait until next week before booking anything.

It was all getting too complicated for Ilma, and it was time for her to make a decision.

Ilma got up and poured herself another gin and tonic, trying to focus on the future. Can I get Rod to come and live here with me? Probably not, he is still a young man, who will want to enjoy himself in the company of friends, play tennis and generally get involved in things, she thought to herself. What would he do in Dareboolah? He would not last a week. No, I have to get him to go away with me, to live somewhere at least as big as Sandhaven Creek. Perhaps Armidale or Tamworth or even Brisbane, somewhere we can both get jobs.

But he will ask what we will live on in the meantime, and I will have to have some sort of answer, she continued to think to herself. Well, I do have a little bit of my own money left, maybe $12,000 in the term deposit, and I could sell the gallery business or I could raise a mortgage on the buildings. How lucky I bought them outright with the money I got from Dad's estate. But all this will take time. Perhaps I can sell the stock to Nardia and rent out the buildings to her. I wonder how much I could ask for the stock? The gallery collection is worth about fifteen thousand, but I suppose I would be lucky to get half this amount from Nardia. I guess eventually I will get a reasonable share of whatever assets I own jointly with Vince, but I don't want to push him on it. After all, Vince has been good to me, and it is not his fault I have fallen in love with Rod.

It was not Vincent's fault, although he had changed considerably since they were first married. They used to get away together a lot. They had some good times at Tamworth at the weekends, and in Sydney or Brisbane during the school holidays. They would go to the theatre, to dances, and to good restaurants. Then it all changed when he became school Principal. All those meetings he had to attend. There were evening sessions with concerned parents and bargaining time with local business people to attract sponsors. They had to stay in Sandhaven Creek during the holiday periods and it became more and more difficult to free up time.

And of course, two years ago, he was silly enough to put up his hand for the social club Presidency, which had limited their time out together to only a few hours a week playing tennis, and one or two evenings at the social club. Still, Ilma did encourage him at the time.

No, I can not blame Vince, and I don't want to take all his money, she thought. For a while Rod and I will just have to survive on the term deposit money. If I transfer it to my bank account tomorrow, I will only lose about $60 in interest. So maybe I should do this. Get the money freed up and into my own account. Oh, and there is about $4000 in the gallery account, she remembered. She could use this as well.

Poor Vincent. She did feel sorry for him. But what could she do? Now she was in love with Rod I would have to leave Vincent anyway. It would not be fair to him to stay on, and in any case, she could not see herself keeping the secret for much longer. But how would she tell him? It was not going to be easy. Oh well, what has to be, has to be. But first I have to convince Rod going away together and starting a new life is the only way for them. She continued to get lost in her own thoughts. We could not stay in Sandhaven Creek, I couldn't live while knowing everyone was talking about us and whispering behind my back.

Rod will be here soon. God, I cannot wait to have him touch me. He is such a good lover, I wonder where he learnt all his tricks. I had better get some food ready, he will be hungry when he arrives. And some champagne, to get him in the right mood to talk. Oh, and where did I put the new packet of fragrant soap. It must still be in my handbag.

★

At ten minutes past eleven, having just finished showering, and dressed only in a shower robe, Ilma opened the apartment door to let Rod in.

"Come in, Gypsy," she said, putting her arms around his neck, kissing him, pushing her body hard against him, then swinging him around and kicking the door shut.

"Wow, this is some greeting," said Rod, at the end of her embrace.

"Well, I've been waiting a whole week for this moment. We're going to have a lovely night, my love. We have champagne and smoked salmon and crayfish, for starters, then you get me for a main course. You can have a little peek if you like, just to wet your appetite," and she opened her bathrobe to reveal her nakedness for a moment, then closed it again and took Rod's hand. "Come on, sit down, we have to talk first." She looked at Rod, gave a nervous little laugh, poured two glasses of champagne and handed one to him.

Ilma took a deep breath, and blurted out, "The thing is, Rod. The thing is, well, I'm in love with you, terribly in love with you, my dear Gypsy." Her voice softened as she continued, "I want to be with you all the time, not just once a week. And I want to be able to show you off and talk about you to people. It's not right we have to hide our feelings for each other from public scrutiny, we should be able to celebrate and tell the world. No Rod, don't stop me, let me finish. I've been thinking. I have some money, not much, but enough to go on until we find work. We can be together, Rod. We can make a new life. There is enough money to buy a small business somewhere. Oh Rod, just think how nice it would be, we could live in Toowoomba or Brisbane, or somewhere up on the north coast. Somewhere we can do exciting things together. You don't really want to live in Sandhaven Creek for the rest of your life, do you? Let's do it, Rod, let's go away together, I love you, I do love you."

Ilma stopped talking and kneeled in front of Rod, resting her hands on his knees. "Will you? Will you, Rod?" she whispered.

Ilma gazed at him in what she believed was an adoring fashion, but Rod interpreted it as a pleading look. He was embarrassed and more than a little fearful. He was not about to give her a truthful answer as he didn't want the confrontation it would bring. "Oh, well, hmmm," he stuttered.

He is silent for a moment, then he recovers his wits

and puts together a plausible story which he hopes will enable him to avoid a direct answer. "Well, of course it would be great to be together, and I have thought about us going away but, you know, there is a lot to consider. My job for instance, I quite like working at The Journal, and I get on very well with Joe. Maybe if I just had more time to think it through. Maybe, like, I could think about living in Tamworth and driving to Sandhaven Creek every day. It's not so far, there are people in Melbourne and Sydney who take much longer to get to work. Let's give it a bit of time, love, sort of kick it around a bit. Maybe I could keep my eye open for a flat to rent in Tamworth."

Rod's reasoning didn't convince her. She made a further attempt to persuade him it is time, for the love she believed they have for each other, to be out in the open. She urged, "But Rod, Vince will find out about us sooner or later, I know. And I cannot live like this much longer. I feel guilty, Rod. Right now, only my love for you is keeping me going. Please don't let what we have between us, wither away because we feel guilty and frightened every day. Please, Rod, please."

Rod could tell she was wheedling him rather than arguing with him, so he stood firm. More confidently he assured her, "I want to, love, honest. Let me think about it over the weekend. Maybe we can make up an excuse to have a coffee together on Monday morning. I know what. You can tell Vincent I want your advice in regard to an article I'm writing on local artists and how they present their work. He'll see nothing wrong in me seeking your advice, and we can meet freely. Tell him I phoned you about it yesterday."

Ilma, torn between her fears and her desires, let the matter rest for the moment. She was confident Rod would soon come to the right decision. After all, she thought, leaving Sandhaven Creek together is the only way of continuing their relationship, and of avoiding a confrontation between Rod and Vincent. A confrontation she was sure Rod did not want.

Satisfied Rod was close to agreement, Ilma was willing to drop the subject for a while. There was too much promise of sexual gratification to risk spoiling everything. Patting Rod's knee she reassured him. "It's alright Rod, I know this is a bit sudden. But you will think about what I'm saying, won't you? I mean, you do want us to be together, don't you?

"Of course I do, you know I do," said Rod in a now steady voice, trying to sound as sincere as possible.

Ilma leaned her head against his shoulder and runs a finger over his lips. "Monday then, I'll wait until Monday."

They were quiet for a minute or two then Rod said, "Shall we eat now, or shall I prove my love to you in the best possible way?"

Ilma got to her feet. "Oh Rod, in the best possible way," she said, and added with a grin, "but let's take some champagne with us."

It was unfortunate for Ilma she was unaware of Rod's real thoughts as he picked up the champagne bottle. He didn't want to be tied down, and he was getting bored with Ilma's romancing. He thought this may have to be the last time he shared her bed, and he wanted to make the most of it.

The next morning, under the pressure of Ilma's passionate pleas, and anxious to get away from them, Rod agreed to start the hunt for a flat in Tamworth. However, to protect himself, he warned Ilma it could take at least a month to find something suitable. Enough time he hoped to cool things down between them.

★

Later in the day Ilma was sitting on a sofa at home, waiting for Vincent to come and join her for their ritual Friday pre-club drink. She had convinced herself Rod was now accepting her proposal for them to live together, and it was only a matter of time before they do. She began to wonder how best to make the separation from Vincent, and how and when to tell him their marriage was over.

If I tell him now, she thought, what will he do? Will he tell me to leave straight away? If he does, I suppose I can go and stay at the gallery for a few days, until Rod has made up his mind where we may live. But what will Vince do? He will probably be too upset to go to the club, and he loves his Friday nights. Oh, why do I have to do this to him?

Maybe I should not tell him until tomorrow, but then it will spoil his tennis. Oh, and then later we are all going to the exhibition at the Town Hall. Oh God, there is no right time to tell someone you are going to leave them. And how do I tell him? Do I just come out and say, "Vince, I am in love with Rod and we are going away together," or should I take a softer line and say, "Vince, I want a little breathing space, I am thinking of going away for a while, it's not your fault, but I am getting a bit bored in Sandhaven Creek," and then maybe, after a few weeks, I could just let it be known I am not coming back. A bit of a coward's way out but it does have some advantages, it would not be so hard on him, and it would enable me to make some better financial arrangements.

Ilma then thought about writing to him instead. Maybe she would wait until Monday and then just go, leaving him a letter and wishing him well. Yes, of course. Perhaps it is the best way, because I can tell him I want us to still be friends, she decided. But if I tell him tonight I am leaving him, we will both get terribly emotional, and it may finish up with a bitter ending to our marriage. I do not want this. Oh, what a mess. What do I do?

She thought about Rod. What if on Monday morning he tells her he wants them to live in Brisbane but needs more time to organise it. She could not tell Vincent anything while Rod was still living in Sandhaven Creek. She had better wait and see what Rod had to say before deciding when to tell Vince.

She heard footsteps. Vincent entered the room and sat next to her. Quietly he said, "Hello dear. You're looking glum, are you tired?"

"Yes," she replied. "And I have a headache. I'm sorry, Vince, really I am. I know this is the second time this month, but would you mind if I again take a rain check on going out tonight? I am tired, and we do have a busy day tomorrow."

She looked at Vincent, and pulled a funny face. "The exhibition, remember?"

"Oh yes, at the Town Hall. What time is the opening?"

"I think about six thirty. But Vince, I can't finish this drink. I'll have to go and lie down. No, don't worry, it's just a headache. I've had too much to think about at the gallery."

Ilma got up and went towards the bedroom. I'll see Rod tomorrow at tennis, she thought. Maybe he will have already made up his mind.

★

Making news, Saturday 17 May 1997:
Kim Hyung Chui, the second son of South Korean President Kim Young Sam, was arrested today on bribery and tax evasion charges.

Comment:
It was doubtful anyone in Sandhaven Creek could get away with bribery or tax evasion – they knew each other too well.

At four o'clock on Saturday afternoon, Ilma walked off the tennis court. As she passed the next court she called to Vincent, who was playing in a mixed doubles game, "Vince, what's your score? We'll have to get away soon, it's just after four on my watch."

"I shan't be long. We've just started a tie-breaker."

"Okay. I'll wait here with Rod."

About ten minutes earlier, Rod had finished playing in a set with three other club members and was sitting on a bench near to Vincent's court. Ilma was annoyed she had not been able to be with him all afternoon and now he had chosen to sit where they would be unable to talk freely. With pent up emotion and a thumping heart she sat down beside him, leaving some space between them. She clearly wished to hold his hand and sit closer to him, but she knew she must not yet advertise her feelings for him. Their secret must be kept for a little while longer.

"Hi," she said quietly. Then looking at an envelope he was holding, "What have you there? Is your Bank Manager writing you a love letter?"

Rod folded the envelope and slipped it into his tennis bag. "I picked up my mail on the way home, I just remembered it but I haven't opened it yet, I think it's a letter from my brother, he often uses a typewriter. I'll read it later."

Ilma thought Rod's voice sounded a little flat, but with Vincent so near, Ilma realised it would be unwise to be drawing Rod into any sort of conversation of a personal nature. She felt uneasy sitting next to Rod and not being able to touch him. She knew, from earlier talk around the table at afternoon tea, Rod was going to be at the exhibition, so she decided to try to get a quiet moment with him there.

Shortly, feeling she could sit next to him for no longer without embracing him, she got to her feet. "See you at the exhibition then, Rod," she said, trying to sound casual and talking loud enough to ensure at least a couple of players hear her, "I'm going to freshen up." She had hoped Rod would follow her into the pavilion, but he didn't. When she came out again he had gone.

★

Making news, Saturday 17 May 1997:
'Modulations and Permutations', an exhibition of etchings, paintings and sculptures held at The Williams Gallery in Princetown, will close at 5pm.

Comment:
A quite different art exhibition opened today in Sandhaven Creek. At the exhibition, all the better known town citizens were quaffing the gallery's wine and talking about something other than the paintings.

From a sales point of view, Florian's exhibition may be quite successful, thought Ilma, as she threaded her way through the crowd in the Town Hall ballroom. Around her were the sixty-two paintings making up the exhibition, some mounted on a number of large display screens, and the remainder hanging on the ballroom walls. She could see the colours of his paintings were not so harmonious as his earlier works, and the brush strokes were nowhere near as deft.

Ilma was aware she was attracting attention. She was aware she didn't have the prettiest face in the world but she knew how to dress to show off her other attractions. She was wearing a loose flowing royal blue satin mid-length dress, off the shoulders except for two very thin blue cord straps, and free of any pattern or adornments. Her bare and tanned legs were supported on high-heeled white leather open sandals with ankle straps.

Her hair was swept up and tied with a blue ribbon, and

she had a small diamond pendant hanging from each ear. She carried a glass of champagne in her right hand and was straining on tiptoe, looking for Rod.

Instead she saw Florian, and even above the crowd noise she could hear his voice, and she could tell he'd had too much to drink. Less than an hour after the opening speeches, and already he was drunk, she thinks. And she wondered how he ever stayed sober enough to paint. And looking at these recent paintings of Florian's, she was not so sure he did. She watched him fling out an arm in a gesture towards a portrait painting, and in doing so, knock a glass of champagne out from the hand of a rather small young lady of somewhat staid appearance. In his attempt to slur out 'sorry' he sprayed out a mouthful of white wine all over the sleeve of her elderly companion, and then weaved his way across the room to join another group of people.

She was not the only one watching Florian's progress. Several pairs of eyes were upon him, including those of Phillip Jackson, who had already discreetly taken a number of photos.

As Florian swayed to a stop, Ilma saw Rod over near the foyer door talking to Vincent, and she decided it would be unwise to approach Rod at this moment. She saw Jan nearby and moves in her direction, but found Contessa Ralstone standing in her path. "Looking for someone?" asks Contessa.

"Oh, not really," replied Ilma. "I am Just eyeing the field."

"Florian has been busy. He must have used a lot of paint."

"And canvas," Ilma chuckled. "He's obviously into his 'big is beautiful' period. Which is why he's exhibiting here, I guess. Small galleries like mine can only have a few of his paintings these days, not like his first exhibition with me, I hung over thirty of his paintings then, but of course, none were larger than Margaret Preston's 'Native Flower', of which there is a very good quality print in the local library, if you remember?"

"Yes. We talked about it when we met there last year. As I recall it's only about five hundred x four-fifty. But why did you mention Margaret Prestons painting?"

"Well, Florian's early work was of similar style. He used to say he would like to paint like her."

A waitress with a tray of tiny cocktail sausages interrupted them. Ilma picked one up and took a bite, which represented half the sausage. Contessa declined one and politely waited for Ilma to finish hers. Then she asks, "Tell me, honestly Ilma, how do you like his present work? Don't you find it all a bit commercial?"

Ilma licked her fingers. "Yes, I think you're right," she replied. "In fact, it would be true to say I don't like them very much. But I'll bet most will sell. He has a reputation now, and a painters reputation is everything when it comes to selling."

"Do you ever paint, yourself?"

"No. Maybe I'll take it up one day. But actually, I get a lot of pleasure just having an art gallery and reading a lot of art books. I suppose I paint through other people's hands and eyes," Ilma laughed. "And I don't have to clean up afterwards."

Contessa looked thoughtful "I sometimes wonder about my sculpture," she said. "Is it worth all the mess I make when I am working? I think Rodin must have had an apprentice to keep his studio clean."

Ilma saw Vincent approaching and thought she may now be able to talk to Rod. She motioned Vincent to join them and introduced him into the conversation. "Contessa and I have been talking about Florian's paintings. We both agree he seems to be getting more interested in quantity rather than quality. What do you think, Vince?"

"Well, they are big, for sure," Vincent laughed. "I've never been a fan of Florian's," he said, "so I don't think I'm qualified to talk about his paintings in any helpful way. Personally, I prefer looking at small watercolours. I find them softer on the eye and, I think, more subtle."

"Why Vincent," exclaimed Contessa. "You surprise me. I didn't know you to be so discerning. Most men like big brash paintings. The macho thing, you know. Large status symbols; all those imaging sort of things."

Vincent laughed again, "I get all my macho out of my system on the tennis court, but it doesn't do me much good when I play against Brian. And what are you doing, Contessa? You're not going to turn into another Henry Moore, are you? You have too much talent to be producing raw symbolism. You can actually produce life-like pieces."

Ilma allowed the conversation between Vincent and Contessa to develop, then thinking the two of them to be sufficiently engaged, she announced she needed to find the little girl's room.

She could see Rod still standing near the foyer door. He appeared to be on his own. She headed off towards the foyer and as she passed him she quietly said, "Follow me in a minute, I'll be in the writing room."

The foyer was quite large, and apart from a couple walking through, it was empty of people. On her left, a wide stairway led up to the Council Chambers. On her right were three doors, one marked 'ladies', one marked 'gentlemen' and another, marked 'writing room'. Ilma opened the writing room door and, as she expected, found the room unoccupied. She entered and sat down to wait for Rod.

Rod was in no hurry. He was reluctant to again be pressured into giving everything up for Ilma. Today was the first time he had been to a gallery opening night, and he liked the atmosphere. In fact, he is getting to like living in Sandhaven Creek and being accepted into its social set. He was beginning to feel more relaxed in the company of intellectual women like Sally and Jan and Contessa, and to appreciate the level of conversation he got while having a drink with Brian and Vincent, especially Brian, from whom he had learnt about local history and politics. Their relatively sophisticated world was all new to him, and he wanted to be part of it.

On the other hand, he knew Ilma would catch up with him at some point in the evening and realised he could not afford to ignore her. The risk of getting her angry in front of everyone was too great. If she went on here as she did at the Post Office that day, all eyes would be on them – including Vincent's. Better to keep her calm and talk to her in private, rather than finish up quarrelling in public, even if he has to endure an ear bashing for a few minutes, he thought. Ilma must understand there was danger in them both leaving the exhibition hall at the same time, especially if it was for a longer period of time than the natural call of nature requires.

Reluctantly he turned away from the exhibition's attractions and the attendant crowd and went into the foyer to find the writing room. Crossing his fingers, he reached for the door knob.

Ilma got up, closed the door and pulled him to her. "Oh Gypsy," she whispered. "It was awful at tennis today, sitting next to you and not being able to touch you. Please tell me we'll soon be together." Before he could say anything, she maneuvered him over towards a large writing table and started kissing him passionately.

Edging around as she was kissing him, she positioned herself so her bottom was touching the table. She stopped kissing him for a moment, while she unbuttoned his shirt and slipped an exploring hand inside. She heard Rod's protests but didn't take them in. She leaned back and flicked the support straps off her shoulders and wriggles her body to enable the top of her dress to fall to her waist. She wore no bra or undergarment. She could see the mix of excitement and fear on his face. "No," he said, his voice nearly breaking. "Someone may come in. And anyway, Ilma, it all..."

But she didn't let him finish. She draped her arms around his neck and kissed him again, exerting surprising strength to pull his body forward until he was nearly on top of her as she leaned backwards over the table edge. She drew her mouth away and said, "It's alright, Gypsy, it's alright. Nobody is going to come in here."

He grabbed her shoulders and she thought he understood what had to be. But he tensed and hissed, "Stop it. There is someone in the foyer."

Trying to kiss him, she said, "It's only some guys going for a pee." Rod straightened his arms, not allowing their mouths to make contact. She thought he was at last playing the male dominant role and she reached for the buckle of his trouser belt. She undoes the buckle and pulls on his trouser zip. It jams half way down and she struggles with it.

The writing room door burst open and Florian stood swaying in the doorway. "Where's the bloody toilet?" he boomed, peering around and then comprehending the room was occupied. "Ooh, it's Dolly Dolly. Ooh, ye are avin a good time. Wash ya doin' in the mens loo? Ooh, I know wash ya doin'. Naughty Dolly."

Standing in the doorway next to Florian was Brian. Behind Brian was Vincent and another man. And behind them all was Phillip Jackson – a camera raised above Vincent's shoulder and emitting two quick flashes. Vincent looked like he had been momentarily turned to stone.

Brian was struggling with Florian. "Come on, you silly fool, get out of here, the toilet's next-door."

Rod broke away from Ilma, trying to fix up his trousers. "Oh God," he said. "What now?"

With a heaving chest Ilma pulled her dress into place, all the time looking beyond Florian and Brian, and straight at Vincent. For a moment she held his eye, then Vincent turned and walked away. Brian, with the other man's help, escorted Florian from the room, allowing the door to close behind him.

Hurriedly Ilma said, "I'll have to go, Rod. I can't do this to Vincent in front of his friends, without telling him I'm sorry. He has to know I care at least a little bit for him." She softened her voice, "But it's all in the open now, Gypsy, we can plan for the future. Tonight I'll tell Vince I am leaving him."

Rod was now slumped in the waiting room chair. "Well I…"

But again Ilma interrupted him, "Tomorrow, Rod, tomorrow. I'll see you in the morning."

She quickly went into the foyer, leaving Rod still sitting in the chair and muttering, "Oh hell."

Ilma could hear Florian attempting to sing in the men's toilet, but there was nobody in the foyer. She went into the ballroom and searched for Vincent. He was not to be seen. She saw Contessa and asked her if she had seen Vincent, but Contessa only told her Vincent went to help Brian get Florian to the men's room. Ilma thought Vincent may have gone outside to cool off, so she went back through the foyer and out into the street. There was no sign of Vincent so she turned to the left and walked into the car park. The space in which they had parked their car was empty. Suddenly she became overwhelmed as she realised her old life was now over. There would be no Vincent to look after her, no comfortable house to live in, and probably no friends. She was determined to make a new life with Rod. But for now, the emotion of it all was too much, and she just sat on the ground and cried.

She cried for about fifteen minutes before the sobbing slowly abated. She got to her feet to see Jan and Brian coming towards her. Jan touched her arm and said, "Oh Ilma, you poor thing. We've been looking all over the place for you. Brian told me about Florian. What an idiot, opening the door on you and Rod. You didn't choose a very safe place, did you? Whatever were you thinking about? But there, I can see you're too distressed to talk about it now. Brian says Vincent has gone home."

Looking concerned and uncomfortable, Brian said, "I'm sorry, Ilma, Vincent isn't taking it very well. I followed him from the building and he gave me a message for you. He said he'll leave some money and your car keys in the letterbox, and put your car in the street. He says he doesn't want to see you tonight, he'll see you in the morning. He would prefer you to sleep at Dareboolah tonight."

Brian continued, "I'm sorry I had to tell you this, Ilma, but I promised Vincent I would. I said we'd run you over to pick up your car. But seeing you like this, I don't think you should be driving anywhere tonight in the state you're in. I think you should come and stay with us overnight, and take a fresh look at things in the morning."

Jan put a comforting arm around Ilma's shoulders. "Yes, Brian's right. You should come with us, and maybe it'll help if you and I have a heart to heart talk."

Ilma tried to recover her composure. "Have either of you seen Rod?" she asked.

Brian replied, "I passed him when I got back to the foyer after saying goodbye to Vince. He nodded to me and

I said something quite inane, like 'bad luck'. He didn't stop. He left the building quickly and I saw him turn right so I think he may have parked his car down near the Post Office or perhaps in Harvey Street. He'll be back at the caravan now, or he may have gone for a walk or a drive to steady his nerves. He would have to be worried as to how Vincent is going to react."

It dawned on Ilma Vincent may react very badly, and given Vincent's size, Rod may be in danger. She fastened onto Brian's arm and looks at him pleadingly. "Please," she gasped, "I have to find Rod. I have to know he is somewhere safe. I have to warn him Vincent may come looking for him. I don't want Rod injured, and I don't want Vince to go to jail."

★

In the exhibition hall, Sally approached Contessa Ralstone who was standing alone in front of a painting. "Hi Contessa. Have you seen Brian? I hear there has been some trouble with Florian."

Contessa wrinkled her nose in distaste. "Yes," she acknowledged. "Florian is so drunk he's been pawing a few women. Brian and Vincent and Vincent's friend, Tom, have taken him away to sober him up. I doubt he will be back. The opening formalities will have to proceed without him."

Thoughtfully Sally had a sip of wine before asking, "Has Ilma gone with them, do you know?"

"No. I don't think so," Contessa replied, and she smiled. "Actually, she and I and Vincent were talking, and she sort of drifted off while Vincent and I started discussing watercolours. I hardly noticed her departure." Then, as if it had suddenly dawned upon her, she said in a confidential manner, "Do you know Sally, Vincent is more knowledgeable about paintings than I ever imagined. Some of his views are interesting."

"Oh," said Sally quietly. "Vincent is knowledgeable about many things." She would like to have added 'except for women', but she refrained.

Brian's friend came over to join them. Sally was not sure whether he was addressing Contessa or herself, but he announced, "Bloody Florian. He has really done it this time. We were trying to get him to the toilets and he broke away from Brian and I, and he opened the wrong door. And on the other side was our young reporter fellow having it off with Ilma."

He looked, first at Contessa, and then at Sally, then in a lower voice he continued. "Ilma was nearly naked, and Vincent was in the foyer and saw the whole thing."

Sally's heart fluttered. She was hearing the sort of news she had wanted to hear for a long time. Yet she knew Vincent would be hurt if what she was being told is true. "What about Vincent?" she asked.

"What about Ilma?" asked Contessa.

No one asked him about Rod.

★

In the car park Ilma was getting all worked up and verging on hysteria. Jan grabbed her shoulders and vigorously shook her. "Don't be silly, Ilma," she said in a firm voice and showing signs of annoyance. "If you're worried about Rod we can go to the caravan and see if he's there, although I suspect he is probably laying low and out of sight."

She paused for breath, having been speaking quickly in order to break through Ilma's hysteria. Keeping up the pace, she continued. "It doesn't matter how you feel about Rod, it's Vincent who matters to us at the moment. We're not going to judge you, Ilma, it's your life. We'll always be your friends, but Vincent is our friend too, and I wouldn't like to see you upset him further, through doing something you may regret in the morning. If Rod has any feelings for you he'll understand this, and he'll wait for you to sort things out with Vincent before you see him again."

Slowing down a little, Jan said more softly, "You know you haven't been very clever. We were pretty sure you and Rod were having an affair, we've seen the way you look at him and we saw you and Rod together last Monday. We had hoped you'd get over it before Vincent found out, but now he has, I think you should show him a little loyalty, at least until you've faced up to him."

Ilma calmed down and took a deep breath. Her mind was all mixed up and getting nowhere. She really wasn't thinking straight and she blurted out, "Oh Jan. I don't want to hurt Vince, and I don't want to lose your friendship. But I'm in love with Rod, and it's too late for me to deny it. I hear what you say, and if Rod is not at the caravan, I'll very gratefully come back to your place for the night. But tomorrow I'll be telling Vincent I'm leaving him."

Jan and Brian looked at each other, trying to come to grips with what Ilma was saying, then Brian said, "Come on, Ilma, let's get you home. The car is over there, in the next row."

On the way home Brian stopped at the caravan park, but Rod was not at home. At Ilma's request he put a note on the caravan door, to inform Rod Ilma will be there in the morning at about eleven o'clock.

Arriving home, Jan showed Ilma to a guest room, where for a while they sat and talked about the situation Ilma was in. Jan then made Ilma a strong cup of cocoa, handed her a couple of sleeping tablets and bedded her down for the night. She stayed with Ilma until she became drowsy then tiptoed out.

Brian was waiting for her in the kitchen. He had two gin and tonic drinks poured out.

"Is she asleep?" He asked, passing one over.

Jan nodded. "Yes," she answered. "She was quite exhausted. I feel really sorry for her, but oh, how could she do this to Vincent, or to all of us really. It is so selfish of her."

"Love is blind, I suppose. Although what she can see in Rod totally escapes me. He seems to me to be a pretty immature young man, and penniless as well. She surely won't want to live with him in the caravan; it would soon lose any romantic flavour."

Brian took a gulp of his gin and tonic. "Hell," he said, meaningfully. "I've just remembered Florian. We left the silly old goat laying on the toilet floor sleeping like a baby. I hope Tom doesn't think I am still in there looking after him." Brian considered going back to the Town Hall. He discussed the idea, and with relief in his voice he said, "Oh well, I suppose someone will have found him, they could hardly miss him, and there was nothing wrong with him except for the booze."

Jan smiled at him, saying, "Yes. I think you can leave Florian to someone else." She sat down and sipped her drink. It relaxed her a little but she was worried about her conversation with Ilma, and needed some reassurance. She confided in Brian.

"Ilma says they are going away together, possibly to Brisbane, or Sydney, whichever presents the best job prospects for Rod."

"Maybe things will look different to her in the morning," Brian cautioned.

"Hopefully," Jan said, widening her eyes. "But, what about Vincent? What do you think he will do?"

"Do you mean if she runs off with Rod? Or if she comes to her senses?"

"Both. I mean what do you think he will do, in either event?"

Brian sensed Jan's fear and thought carefully about his answer. "Well, if she leaves him, I don't think he will go after her, and if Rod goes with her, it will let Rod off the hook. But if she decides to stay with Vince, then my advice to Rod will be for him to leave town quickly."

"Ilma tells me it's not Rod's fault" said Jan. "Apparently it was she who approached him. She told me he reminded her of one of her teenage conquests."

"Hmm. I wouldn't bet on where the guilt lays. Remember you once said he had come to bed eyes."

"I know. And I think he is just stringing Ilma along. She is about ten years his senior and I'll be very surprised if he has any intention of staying with her for any length of time."

There was a pause and Brian said, "I have another thought about all this. What shall we do if Vince tells Ilma to get out, and Rod tells her to get lost?"

"Oh. Do you think it is a possibility?" asked Jan, her eyes widening as if the thought had not occurred to her.

"Yes I do. Vince looked mortally wounded, and Rod looked shocked and scared stiff. It is a combination conjuring up all sorts of outcomes."

Jan looked into her drink for inspiration, then at Brian, "What if we let Ilma stay here for a few days. Give things time to settle down. Would it be disloyal to Vince, do you think?"

"I reckon he would understand our position. We have all been friends for a long time. But the point is, do you want to? Have Ilma stay with us I mean?"

Jan swirled her G&T and gave a wistful smile. "Yes," she said. "I guess we have to give them both as much support as we can, but we have to remember it is Vincent who is the victim in all this."

"Of course, you're right, I had better have a talk with him and explore the possibilities."

Brian squared his shoulders, gulped down the remains of his own G&T, and reached for the telephone.

14
Apologies

Making news, Saturday 17 May 1997:
Laurent Kabila's Rebel forces have taken the city of Kinshasa after Zairian President Mobuto Seso Seko fled the country.

Comment:
Mobuto Seso Seko's world was unravelling, as was Rod Skapleson's.

At about 10.30 p.m., Brian phoned Vincent.

"Vince. Look, I'm sorry about what happened. I thought you'd like to know Ilma is staying here overnight. I had an idea something was going on, but I wasn't sure enough to tell you, and maybe I wouldn't have anyway."

"It's alright, Brian. I know it must have been difficult for you. I'm sure it can't be easy to tell a friend he's being cuckolded."

"It may not be so bad, Vince. You won't do anything rash, will you? I mean, you'll give Ilma a chance to explain herself? It may only be a fling you know, and not necessarily the world's end."

"No Brian, it's more than a fling. I know now why Ilma has been different for the last couple of months. I've had time to think of a number of little incidents which should have told me something was wrong. But I've always been a dummy about relationships. My marriage is over, Brian. I am certain of it. I'm just not sure what I'm going to do about it. I know one thing though, I don't want to be anywhere near Rod in the next few days."

The flat tone of voice used by Vincent frightened Brian. He winced as he imagined the outcome if Vince and Rod met up. Reassuringly, he offered advice. "I don't think you'll need to worry about meeting up with him, Vince. I don't see Rod as the hero type. I'm sure he'll be giving you a very wide berth from now on. Jan says she'll bring Ilma over in the morning at about ten o'clock." There is a silence on the line at the other end, so Brian continues, "Try and patch things up will you, old chum? Jan and I are both concerned for the two of you. We've been friends now for a very long time."

After another moment of silence, Brian heard Vincent's reply, "I'll listen to her, Brian, but I doubt it'll change anything. Sometimes one has to face the facts."

Something in the way he said it worried Brian, and he endeavoured to keep Vincent talking, "What are you doing now?" he asked.

"Having a coffee and watching a documentary on China. And then I'll watch the late night sports show, and afterwards I'll turn over to some stupid reality show, and hopefully fall asleep watching it."

"Would you like some company?"

"Thanks Brian, but no. I have to work through this on

my own. Have a better night than me."

Brian heard the line go dead.

★

Rod got home well after midnight. He had driven to Tamworth and back since leaving the Town Hall. He was physically tired, but not yet ready to sleep. He sat down and picked up the letter he had brought home with him after tennis. He hadn't had time to read before going on to the exhibition.

He looked again at the typewritten address on the envelope, then opened it and took out the letter. It was, as he had thought, from his brother. With growing concern he read the letter.

PO Box 37721
Milson's Point
Sydney NSW 2061

27th March 1996

Dear Rodney,

I have two pieces of news for you. The first item is, I am now residing in Sydney. I am in temporary digs at the moment and looking around for a suitable flat. I will let you know when I find one.

I have been very lucky to get the job of Public Relations Manager with the Sydney based News Mill Group. They employ about two thousand people, and there were a number of internal applicants for the job. So you can imagine I am feeling very pleased with myself. I'll tell you more about the job later, when I fully understand the duties involved. I only started work here on Monday so it will take me a few days, ha ha.

The second, and for you the more important item of news, is I saw Norma before I left Melbourne and she says she is quite determined to get some money out of you one way or another. Now, since she has been trying unsuccessfully to find you for the last couple of months, this may not seem to you to be a worry. However at a Friends party last Saturday I met someone else who may cause you concern. A freelance journalist named Diana Pouchay. The thing is I found out she is coming to stay in Sandhaven Creek for at least a week, to do some investigative journalism about some mystery murders which took place there around the turn of the century. And, wait for it, I am sorry to tell you Diana happens to be an old school friend of Norma's. And she tells me she has been re-igniting the friendship recently, which of course, means she will know Norma's married name, and probably all about you.

Just thought I would warn you, Rod. Hope your job is still to your liking.

Regards,

Andrew

Rod looked again at the letter, but without actually reading it.

"What a bloody awful day," he said out loud.

★

Making news, Sunday 18 May 1997:
New York's news zipper, which for many years flashed headlines to viewers in Times Square, has today closed down. A high-tech electronix version will shortly occupy its place.

Comment:
Sandhaven Creek did not have a news zipper of any kind, but the story of Ilma Mathews' flirtation would no doubt get around the town through word of mouth. It would reach the ears of most citizens within the next few days.

As Ilma stepped out of Jan's car on Sunday morning, she took a deep breath and prepared herself for what she knew would be an emotionally charged meeting with Vincent.

Jan watched Ilma cross the road to her car, which was, as Vince said it would be, parked in the street. Jan saw Ilma stop, look in the letterbox and take out some keys and some money. She watched as Ilma put the money into the small evening purse she had with her at the exhibition. She waited until Ilma had put a key into her house door lock, and then she started her own car and slowly moved off.

Driving home, Jan felt a bit shattered by the night's events, and she was almost glad Brian had told her he needed to be at his office for an hour, to receive some faxes from an overseas client. She did not get much sleep overnight, and was glad to be able to go home and just relax for a while.

She opened the front door as the phone rang. Half

expecting to hear Ilma's voice she rushed over and picked up the receiver.

"Jan Clements here."

"Oh Jan, it's Rod. I… err… about, last night. I suppose Brian has told you what happened."

Vincent and Ilma were both her good friends, and had been for most of her life. Jan did not want to take sides in any argument between them, and at the moment this was a hard enough position to be in. So in her mind Rod was now 'persona-non-grata', and was the last person she had expected to hear from.

When she replied, she stiffened and allowed her anger to come through. In an icy voice she said, "Not only Brian, Rod. We've heard all about your affair from Ilma. She stayed here overnight and she's very upset. I've just dropped her off at her home, but from what I can see it's not likely to be her home for very much longer, thanks to you."

"Jan, I'm sorry, it's not all my fault. Ilma has been throwing herself at me. Look, can I speak to Brian please, there's something I want to tell him. It's important, Jan, very important."

"Well, he's at the office for a while, Rod. I'll tell him you called, you can ring again later." Feeling she may lose her temper entirely, she hung up the phone.

★

Brian called in at the newsagents to buy a Sunday paper. He had a bit of a browse around the shop, and bumped into two of his clients who kept him talking for a while.

Leaving the shop, he then drove on up to his office and was surprised to find Rod's car parked outside, with Rod sitting in it. Rod got out of his car and approaches him. He had a couple of envelopes in his hand.

Brian looked at Rod. His untidy appearance suggested to Brian he was correct in his description of Rod. He really was a rather immature young man, and he probably didn't have two dollars in his pocket to rub together. Despite his own anger at what has happened, he found himself suddenly feeling sorry for this nervous looking and obviously sleep deprived youngster whom he had been befriending.

Rod plucked up the courage to speak, "Hello Brian, can I talk to you for a few minutes?"

Brian's body tensed but he tried to keep his anger under control. "Rod," he said, in as calm a voice as he could muster. "If it's about last night, I really don't want to know any more than I already do."

Rod was not going to be put off. Shuffling his feet he positiond himself in Brian's path and pleaded with him. "Well, it's not just about last night, Brian. I'm sorry about what you saw, and I'm sorry about getting you involved because I know you're Vincent's best friend. But there is something else I want to tell you, and I want to show you a letter."

Brian's curiosity was aroused, and the contrition in Rod's voice released some tension Brian felt in his presence. Gently pushing past Rod he then motioned him towards the office doorway, saying, "I suppose you had better come on in then."

They entered the building together and Brian pointed

to his room. "Go in and take a seat. I'll be with you shortly. I'll make some coffee."

This wass not intended as a friendly act on Brian's part. The truth was Brian felt he needed the coffee to calm himself down. He knew the discussion with Rod would be an uncomfortable experience and it would be hard for him to maintain self-control. He made two instant coffees and put the two cups, some sugar, and a couple of spoons on a tray and carried them to his desk. "No milk, I'm afraid," he said flatly, "Hope you can drink it black."

"Yes, thanks. I didn't expect this," replied Rod, sipping at the coffee gratefully.

"It's for me really, Rod. I feel I'm going to need it. Now what is it you want to tell me?"

Rod slid an envelope across the desk. "Please read this first, Brian," he said.

Brian reads the letter, and then gives Rod a challenging look. "Why am I reading this Rod?" he asked.

Rod looked uncomfortable and slumped back in his chair. With his eyes focused on a photo of Jan on Brian's desk, he said, "I don't know why." He turned his eyes to Brian, "Maybe," he continues, "it's because you and Jan took me to the club for dinner."

Brian held out the letter, "Do I take it from this Norma is your wife, or perhaps your ex-wife?" he asked.

"I'm married to Norma, but I don't think of her as my wife any more. She's a high-flyer. A career woman who will do anything to get what she wants. I just couldn't keep up with her. I did a bunk and I didn't tell her where I was going. She wants money I haven't got, to pay for a house we didn't need. And when she finds out where I am she'll give me a lot of legal hassle, for nothing except spite. I haven't told Ilma. Ilma has got it into her head we're going to live together. I have never agreed to it. Ilma was finding life dull, and she wanted a bit of excitement. She chose me to give it to her. It wasn't supposed to be a big deal. We were just to meet at her flat at the gallery on Thursday nights, and nobody was to know. Least ways, this is how I saw it. But it wasn't long before Ilma wanted more, and she convinced herself I did too. Well, I didn't, and I tried to tell her yesterday, but she kept smothering me. And just as I was about to force her to listen to me, bloody Florian, mucked everything up."

"So what happens now, Rod? Right at this minute it's probable either Ilma is now telling Vincent she's leaving him, or Vincent is telling her to get out."

"I don't think there's anything I can do about it, Brian. I don't want to see Ilma again, it won't do her any good, it won't do me any good, and it won't do Vincent any good either. Anyway, I'm leaving Sandhaven Creek. My car is all packed and ready, and I'll be on my way in a few minutes. I can't risk the journalist woman coming to town and recognising me, so I might as well go now, it'll be better for everyone."

Brian looked at him speculatively and thought there was no point in arguing with him. He was too scared to stay around and he didn't have the guts to see Ilma before he left. He wondered what it is Rod wanted, apart from perhaps some sympathy. He pushed the letter away and kept his voice flat. "Well, it's your life, Rod," he declared.

"I'm not going to tell you how to live it. Here, you had better take this letter back."

Rod picked up the letter, folded it, and stuffed it into a pocket. "There's something else though," he said, putting the second envelope on the desk. "I would really appreciate it if you'll give this to Joe Bernaldo for me, I can't find him and he isn't answering his phone. The envelope contains the keys to the office and to the caravan, and a short letter to Joe. It's to tell him I'm leaving and why, and to thank him for all his help, particularly in buying the van. And it's to let him know he can sell the caravan for whatever he can get for it and keep the money, and I will forego the few payments I've made on it."

Rod got up and turns towards the door, not waiting for Brian to reply. "I don't expect we'll see each other again," he said, with a bit of a smile returning to his face. "You'll probably be pleased to see the back of me, but I'd like you to know I appreciated the friendship you all extended to me, and I think I would have liked to settle down in Sandhaven Creek."

"Good luck, Rod," said Brian, rising to his feet as Rod departed without further ado.

I'm not sure I wanted to shake his hand anyway, Brian thought, sitting down again and fingering the envelope addressed to Joe. "I suppose I will have to deliver it personally," he mutters to himself.

Brian recalled his comment last night to Jan. He had suggested he would advise Rod to leave town if Ilma stays with Vincent. Well, Rod didn't wait for his advice, he just assumed Ilma would return to Vincent, and he came to his own conclusion as to the consequences. But when they spoke on the phone, Vincent seemed to be saying his marriage was over and he didn't want to see Rod, so Rod's departure could be premature. Unless of course; these events were not the real reason for Rod's panic. Perhaps it was more to do with his wife chasing him for money he didn't have, and he did not want to owe under a Court Order.

And maybe Vincent could be convinced Ilma's little adventure was not so serious.

Brian imagined Ilma could be suffering from boredom in Sandhaven Creek, she had hinted so on a number of occasions. If Vincent were to take her to the big smoke every so often, she would probably be more content. When things cooled down between them, he thought, he may suggest the four of them take a holiday together.

Brian became lost in thought, trying to predict the consequences of Rod and Ilma's affair, wondering what would happen to Ilma, and worrying about Vincent would do about the situation he was in.

Should he ring Vincent or should he leave him alone for a while? He decided to wait until he got home. It was quite likely Jan would now have an update on the situation.

Brian continued to cogitate, until the fax machine chattering disturbed him. He went over to the machine and plucked out the fax page. He returned to his desk and drafted a suitable reply. It took him a full hour.

Outside, Rod sat in his car for a few minutes, taking in the scene. He turned on the ignition, put the car in gear and drove slowly towards the roundabout where he turned and started his long drive to Sydney. He hoped to find Andrew and see if he could get him a job with the News Mill Group.

★

Entering the house, Ilma was surprised to hear the noise of a vacuum cleaner. She went in the noise direction and found Vincent cleaning the carpet in the guest bedroom. On the way through she noticed all the other carpets had been cleaned. Vincent turned off the vacuum cleaner and looked at her with a set face. "We had better sit in the kitchen," he said, leading the way.

In the kitchen, Vincent pulled out a chair and sat down at the table. In a toneless voice he said, "Well, what do you want to say?"

His demeanour disconcerted her. She had been prepared for Vincent to be angry and to shout at her, but she had not expected this cold indifference from him. It was far worse than him abusing her, either verbally or even physically. It was as if they were total strangers, and nothing she could think of to say would make any difference.

Flustered, Ilma went to a cupboard and took out a bottle and two glasses. "This may help us relax, Vince."

"Pour one for yourself," he said flatly. "I don't need one."

Ilma poured herself a drink, but didn't sit down. Instead she remained standing, leaning her back against the kitchen bench, trying to re-group her thoughts. She needed to be honest with him and to get it all over as soon as possible.

"I'm sorry, Vince. I really don't know what to say." Her voice was charged with emotion. "I just found life was getting on top of me, the same routine every day. I thought I could have a little excitement without hurting you. I'm sorry, I was wrong." She took a deep breath and with steadier voice she continued, "But now it's too late, I've fallen in love with Rod, and I'm going away with him."

Vincent stared at her, his eyes almost looking through her. There was no turning back now. From that moment on there was no Ilma in his life − just emptiness. This woman standing here in front of me is someone I don't know, he thought. Someone I don't want to argue with, someone I don't want to see again.

"Just like that, hey Ilma," he said, the bitterness becoming noticeable. "What is it now, thirteen or fourteen years we've been married? And through it all you've wanted for nothing. I gave everything I had to you, and it wasn't enough, was it? I don't want a wife who gives so little in return and shows no respect. If you want to go off with Rod, just go. There is no need for us to talk about it."

Vincent sat back in his chair. He looked at Ilma and saw the tears in her eyes, and he noticed the tremble of her hand as it holds the drink. For a fleeting moment he was sorry for her and she was again the wife he loved and wanted to protect. But he had spent all night thinking about the scene in the writing room, and what it meant, and his resolve didn't waiver.

In a dismissive way he said, "Look Ilma, it's finished between us. Collect whatever you may need for the next few weeks. You can see Brian to sort out any financial matters which need resolving. I had to go to the garage this morning to pay the account, so I took your car and filled it with petrol. I need the cheque book, but you can take the credit card. Don't take too long packing."

Ilma took a gulp from her glass. She was stunned. She looked around the kitchen, then at Vincent. It's all over, she thought, it's all over and I am not sure I am ready for it. She realised she must now persuade Rod, they would have to stay at least overnight in Dareboolah, so she could make arrangements with Nardia about the gallery future. She slowly breathed in, "I'll get my things together," she said, putting her glass down carefully on the bench.

Without another word, Vincent got up and returned to the guest bedroom to carry on with the vacuuming. When the carpet was clean he put the vacuum cleaner away, got a bucket and some warm water and started to clean the kitchen windows. After this he emptied the kitchen tidy and washed the kitchen floor.

Ilma met him in the hallway. She had two suitcases and a carry bag at her feet. "I'm going, Vince," she said. "I'll have to stay in Dareboolah overnight. I have arrangements to make about the gallery. Phone me if you want." She paused, "Can we be friends?" she asked.

"It's asking a lot, Ilma." The flatness was still in his voice, "Isn't it enough we're not shouting at each other?"

"Then I don't suppose you'll help me to put these in the car?"

"No. I'll carry them as far as the gate, I don't think I want the world to see us parting." Vincent picked up the cases and dumped them just inside the gate. Ilma moved them onto the pavement.

She stood still for a moment, casting her eyes around the garden. "You've been busy this morning, Vince, cut the grass and tidied the flower beds." Then suddenly, with a slight shudder of her body and a lump in her throat, she threw her arms around him, giving him a strong hug and a quick kiss on the cheek. His body was stiff and he made no response. "Goodbye, Vince," she whispered.

Vince turned on his heels and went back into the house. Ilma saw neighbours across the street, looking at her as she packed the bags into her car. She knew they are talking about her. News travelled fast in Sandhaven Creek.

★

Inside the house, Vince made a cup of coffee. There was still a lot to do, he thought. He sat at the table sipping his coffee and wondering, in a detached way, where Ilma and Rod would live, what sort of life she would have with him, and what she would do with the gallery. He pictures the gallery apartment. "And this is where they will sleep tonight," he muttered to himself, bitterly.

He thought of Brian and Jan and Sally, and he was sorry all this is bound to affect them badly. He pictured the birthday party scene and remembered Ilma's speech. She had said we all had her fooled, but he realised now, it was she who had fooled them all. He sighed, and pushed aside the coffee cup.

He went into the living room and took down the fencing foil, "A use for you at last," he muttered, and carried it out to the back terrace, propping it against the wall near the back door. What better way to attract attention, he thought.

He went back to the living room and stood near an open window overlooking the garden. There were some new buds on the roses, he noticed as he closed and locked the window. He stood there for a few moments looking at the garden before turning away.

"I must get on with things," he muttered, returning to the kitchen and gathering up some accounts he had earlier placed in a heap on the table. Taking a cheque book out of a drawer he went through the accounts, making a cheque out for each one. He meticulously recorded each cheque and looked at the balance. There was still a few hundred dollars left over. Satisfied, he went over to the sink and washed his cup and also the glass which Ilma had used. From a corner of a bench he picked up a pair of pliers and a screwdriver which he had used yesterday morning to repair a loose window catch, and he set off for his workshop in the back garden. He paused at the telephone and lifted the receiver off the hook. He didn't want to be disturbed.

In the workshop, he lovingly ran his fingers over a new timber coffee table he had made. "I suppose I have time to give it a finishing coat of varnish," he said to himself, reaching for his dust jacket.

★

At almost exactly eleven o'clock, Ilma pulled into the caravan park. There was no sign of Rod's car. Puzzled, she got out of her own car and walked along the pathway leading to the caravan. As she approached Rod's caravan, she could see the note they left there last night was no longer attached to the door. She knocked on the door and called out, "Rod," but there was no answer. She went to a window and looked in. Nobody there, and no television set, no microwave, no sound system, and almost no books. A cold fear gripped her as she realised Rod may have deserted her. Then the thought came to her – he may have packed up ready to leave with her and then decided to fill up with petrol. In frustration, she bumped on the door with her fist and stood there, nonplussed.

While she was wondering what next to do, the door of a nearby caravan opens, and a tall thin elderly man stepped out and nodded to her. "You looking for Rod?" he called, coming nearer. "You won't find him here, love, he's gone. He took off about a half an hour ago. Nice guy, gave me some books, and sold me a case full of tools real cheap. I guess he needed the money."

"Where has he gone? Did he say?"

"No, love, but last night he came home very late and it woke me up, I mentioned it to him this morning and he told me he'd been to see a friend in Tamworth, and it had got a bit later than he had thought. Maybe he's gone there. He did drive off in its direction."

What to do now. She couldn't go home, it did not exist, and in any case Rod was not going to attempt to contact her there. Nor would he look for her at Jan's place because he wouldn't know she slept there overnight. He was unlikely to come back to an empty caravan, so there was no alternative for her. She would have to go looking for him.

Confused, Ilma went back to her car and sat in it for a minute. She wanted to cry but was also filled with anger. Maybe she was wrong but she felt pretty sure Rod had gone to Tamworth. Probably to see the woman she was told about. Maybe he didn't tell her the truth about being at the market for, what was it? Penance. The only way to find out was to drive to Tamworth and see for herself. But, just in case she was wrong, she decided to drive past the nearest service station and then to drive up Main Street to see if his car was parked near The Journal offices.

Ilma started her car and drove past the service station and on into the Main Street. She drove up and down the street but couldn't see Rod's car anywhere. It was the only thing to do, she thought, speeding up the car and heading off for Tamworth.

While driving along the highway, an idea came to her. Perhaps Rod had mistaken her message and gone to the gallery? The thought bolstered her and she calmed down a little, telling herself it is, after all, quite likely. In better spirits she drove on to the Dareboolah turn off.

At the gallery, however, there was again no sign of Rod, and there were no messages at the gallery to say anyone had been looking for her. In desperation she drove around the streets of Dareboolah searching for his car. She decided to drop off her suitcases at the flat and then drive on to Tamworth.

Entering Tamworth, Ilma headed for Bridge Street and drove along it very slowly until she saw what she believed must be the private hotel. She looked at the few empty car parking spaces in front of the building. She couldn't see Rod's car but she knew there were other parking spaces at the back.

Ilma parked her car at the front, got out, and entered the building. She walked up to the reception counter and pressed the service bell. She was quite agitated and tapped her fingers on the counter top. A minute or so passed and she pressed the bell again, this time giving it several thumps with the palm of her hand. A door marked 'private' opens and Beryl comes to the counter. "Sorry, dear," she said with a grin. "You caught me on the loo. How can I help you?"

Ilma took in Beryl's appearance. A bit older than me, she thought, but quite good looking, about my size and of similar colouring. She was probably the woman Rod had been seen with on market day. She braced herself to remain civil and asked, "I hope I am at the right place. Can you tell me if Rod Skapleson is staying here?"

"He was, dear, but not any more." Beryl could see Ilma was near to breaking point, and she herself is apprehensive as to where this meeting would take them. Nevertheless, she put on a friendly smile, "And I suppose your name is Ilma, I sort of expected you, but not so soon. I'm Beryl, I own this place. Rod may have mentioned me."

Ilma was all tensed up. She hesitated for a moment, unsure of what to do. Beryl looked at her disarmingly. "You had better come in. Come on, I don't bite," she says to Ilma, opening the door marked 'private'.

Ilma followed her through and was amazed at the

room she was entering. It was enormous, about twice the size of her whole flat at the gallery. It had polished redwood floors and pale yellow walls and lots of paintings, hanging in groups. Big windows open out onto a long narrow paved terrace, which had a continuous flower bed backdrop against the property boundary wall. Near the windows, two dark blue wool finished sofas and several blue cushioned cane easy chairs were grouped around the largest coffee table Ilma had ever seen. A round oak dining table with matching chairs, a television and sound system, an oak bookcase and a number of pale blue rugs complete the furnishings. Reluctantly, Ilma admitted to herself, Beryl had class.

Despite her mission and the anxiety, she cannot help acknowledging the pleasantness of her surroundings. "What a nice room," she gasped.

The involuntary remark served to relax them both. Beryl laughed, seeing the incongruity. "Thank you," she replied. She stifled her laugh and continued, "But I am sure you are not here to talk about my room. I guess you want to know where Rod is, and where I fit into things. Well you can put your mind at rest, he is not here and there is nothing going on between us. So you can take it easy for a few minutes and have a seat, and I'll go and make us some tea. And then I'll tell you where I think he may be."

When Beryl left the room, Ilma looked around to see if there was any sign of Rod having been there. Nothing.

Beryl returned, carrying a tray laden with tea and biscuits. She set the tray down and sat in a cane chair.

She looked at Ilma who had taken a seat opposite. "Now," she said, pouring out the tea, "we can have a chat. Rod came here last night. He was very upset and he told me all about your little affair and what happened yesterday. He cancelled his room for next week and he paid me the cancellation fee we had agreed on. He said he had come to collect some things he had left with me, but really I think he just wanted to unburden himself to someone, and I was here. He looked on me as a friend, I don't think he has many."

"Do you know where he is? Did he tell you he was to meet me this morning?"

"Look, dear. I have to say this, although I know it will hurt you. Rod never mentioned you until last night, he obviously isn't in love with you, and he won't be going anywhere with you. He said he's been trying to tell you this for the last couple of weeks, but you kept smothering him and refused to listen. He said he was going to give up his job and go to Sydney. He didn't say when, and maybe I shouldn't have mentioned it."

Ilma got out of her seat, looking out at the garden. Beryl sympathetically looked on in silence. After a minute Ilma turned and looked at Beryl through tear-filled eyes.

"I've been a fool, haven't I? Oh damn him, damn him, damn him for his weakness. He's already gone, you know, taken all his things and gone. He does love me though, I'm sure. He's just a bit scared of taking the plunge."

"I think you're still being a fool, dear." Beryl got up to comfort her. "Face it, love. Rod is not for you. Go back to your husband and try to forget Rod, he's just a very immature young man who will easily forget you and he doesn't want a serious relationship with anyone."

Ilma sat down again. "I can't go back to my husband," she said quietly. "He won't have me back, and I don't deserve him."

Beryl put a hand on her shoulder. "Why don't you go and see," she said.

★

Leaving Bridge Street, Ilma's mind was still in a spin. What to do now? Try to chase Rod and catch up to him before he gets to Sydney? No, she had to accept Beryl had told her the truth. Should she go back to the gallery, or should she take Beryl's advice and try to make up with Vincent?

She drove a little faster, continuing into Greek Road to turn at the roundabout, back to Sandhaven Creek. At the roundabout she was travelling too fast to make the turn. The back wheels of her car skidded around and the car's forward momentum brought her right into line with a large semi-trailer. The crash was unavoidable and she lost consciousness immediately.

★

Brian had just returned home and was anxious to know if Jan had heard from Vincent. But as he closed the door behind him, and before he could ask Jan if Vincent had made contact or tell her about Rod's visit, the phone rang. He waits nearby as Jan answers it.

"Jan, here."

"Mrs. Jan Clements?"

"Yes, I am. Who is speaking?"

"My name is Lucy Perkins. I'm the Charge Nurse at Tamworth Hospital Emergency Ward. I have a patient here, Ilma Mathews. We found her address and phone number in her wallet, and she is wearing a wedding ring. But when I suggested phoning her husband, she became quite hysterical and made it absolutely clear she did not want me to. She gave me your name, said you lived in Sandhaven Creek, and you were the only person I was to ring. She said you would explain everything."

"How is Ilma? What happened?"

"She is in shock still, but she'll be alright. We think she has a broken leg, and maybe some cracked ribs and possibly some minor internal injuries. And she has a lot of cuts and bruises. An ambulance brought her in from an accident at the start of the Oxley Highway. We'll know more about her condition when she's had some x-rays taken. I think though, I can safely say she'll be here for at least a week and will need some personal things to be brought in."

"Oh, yes, I understand. I'll organise a bag for her. You see, she and her husband had a pretty serious argument yesterday and Ilma stayed with us overnight. Understandably she doesn't want you to ring her home number. Can I talk to her please?"

"Not just now. She is in considerable pain and we have her sedated. And she'll probably have to go to theatre when she gets back from x-ray."

"Well, look. When she can understand, will you tell her I'll be there as soon as I can. I'll bring a few obvious necessities with me. Do you know what ward she'll be in?"

"I'm afraid not. You can ask at the reception desk, there will be someone on duty throughout the day. Can I leave it with you then?"

"Of course, and thank you for letting me know."

Jan put down the receiver and turned to Brian. "Some bad news," she said, "Ilma has been in an accident."

"I gathered so. Is she alright?"

"It was a nurse at the hospital speaking. She said Ilma has a broken leg, some cracked ribs and maybe some internal injuries. She's in x-ray now."

Brian looked puzzled. "Which, hospital?"

"Tamworth. I said I'd go and see her and take her some things. Poor girl, as if yesterday wasn't enough. I'll leave in about an hour. Ilma didn't want the hospital to phone Vincent but I think we should tell him, don't you?"

"Yes, I think you're right. I'll ring him now, but I wonder what she was doing in Tamworth. Rod was waiting for me at the office when I arrived. He was packed ready to leave town, but he didn't say where he was going. He did say he didn't want to see Ilma, but he may have changed his mind. The hospital didn't say anything about Rod, did they? Or if there was anyone else injured in the accident?"

"No. I suppose I should have asked."

"What happened when you took Ilma home this morning? Did she and Vincent make it up?"

"I don't know. I just dropped her off and I didn't see her again. I assumed she would either still be trying to sort something out with Vincent, or maybe off somewhere with Rod."

Brian's expression became thoughtful. After a pause he said, "Well, we know now, Rod is on his way to Sydney and he has no intention of ever seeing Ilma again. So it looks like Ilma has been on a wild goose chase as far afield as Tamworth. And it is unlikely she and Vincent have decided to stay together, and work through Ilma's indiscretion."

"I don't often hope you are wrong dear, but with Rod no longer around and given time, they may be able to put the incident behind them. And in a strange way providence may be helping, and maybe Ilma's accident will start the healing process."

"I hope so. But Vince sounded very unforgiving on the phone last night, and I doubt he welcomed Ilma with open arms this morning. This isn't going to be an easy conversation."

Brian picked up the phone and dialed Vincent's number, but couldn't get through. Impatiently, he kept trying every thirty seconds for the next ten minutes. No answer. Frustrated, he decided to give up for a while and try again in another ten minutes.

Jan made a list of some things she thought Ilma may need. She decided she could buy them all at the supermarket. She went into her bedroom and found a couple of pairs of clean pyjamas, a little bit big for Ilma, she thought, but they will do until I collect hers, wherever they may be. She came back to where Brian was sitting and told him she would have to do some shopping on the way, and had better get going.

Brian said goodbye to her and again picked up the

phone, but the result was the same. Knowing Vincent to be a man of few words when on the phone, he suspected the receiver must be off the hook. "I had better go over there," he muttered, picking up his car keys.

★

Arriving at Vincent's house, Brian found the driveway gates were closed. He presumed Vincent must therefore be at home. He parked his car in the road and got out. Opening the smaller pedestrian gate, he took a path leading directly to the front door. He looked at the garden and realised a lot of work had recently been done. He was pleased to think Vincent was busy and keeping his mind off things. He knocked twice on the front door and got no answer. Concluding Vincent must be in his workshop or be tending to the back garden, he walked on past the front door, and along the path leading around the house to the back garden. In the garden he called out Vincent's name, but there was no sign of him. He walked over to the workshop, opened the workshop door and inhaled the smell of fresh varnish. He saw the new coffee table sitting on the work bench. He closed the door without bothering to enter and looked back at the house. At the far end from where he was standing, a door gave access to the house, and another door led to the garage. The new paved terrace linked these two doorways and formed an edge to a well kept lawn.

Brian walked along a short gravel path and stepped onto the paving. The weatherproof covers were on the barbecue and all the garden chairs, and it looked like they have been put to bed for the coming winter. Everything looked very tidy and peaceful, except for a rather sinister new piece of homemade sculpture.

It stood on the garden table, and was made from Ilma's fencing foil. The pointed foil end was buried twenty centimetres into a large soil-filled, but otherwise empty, plant pot. Two bunches of keys were tied to the foil handle. Puzzled, he read the key tags. One indicated school, and the other read S.C.

His heart started to beat faster as he began to realise all was not well. A whiff of something strange caused him to look towards the garage. He could see smoke seeping out from under the garage door. The smell as he approached the garage couldn't be mistaken. It was exhaust fumes.

Brian flung open the door and nearly choked, there was so much exhaust smoke he could hardly see. He pulled a handkerchief out of his pocket, put it over his mouth and nose, and dashed towards the car. A figure was slumped in the driver's seat. He pulled the car door open, reached in and switched off the ignition. He could not see anything clearly, but he had been in Vincent's garage on several occasions and his memory served him well. In an almost continuous movement, he quickly passed the car and pressed the garage automatic door button, and the door began to lift. He got back to the car and recognised the figure was Vincent. Using every ounce of strength he could muster, he pulled Vincent from the car and dragged him away from garage, and onto the front driveway.

Exhausted, he sunk down on his haunches. He thought Vincent was dead and probably had been for some time.

Taking a deep breath, he laid him on his back and went through the routine of mouth to mouth resuscitation and chest pumping. Andy Davies came out of his house to see what was going on. He stepped over the low fence separating the two gardens and came into Brian's line of vision. Brian paused resuscitation efforts long enough to shout, "Get an ambulance, quickly."

Andy turned back towards his house. "Okay, I'll be back soon," he shouted back, and lumbered away, quite fast for a man of his size.

A couple of minutes passed and Brian stopped his attempts at resuscitation. He was exhausted, and he knew it is too late. His friend, Vincent, was dead.

Brian sat on the driveway, beside Vincent's body. There was nothing more he could do.

Andy returned with a blanket which he draped over Vincent's body. He told Brian he had called the ambulance and contacted the police, and then he wandered off into the garage, wafting his hands about to disburse the remaining fumes. He glanced inside the car. On the dashboard was a large photo of Vincent and Ilma cuddling together on a seat in the garden. The surrounding's bareness showed it was taken when they first moved into the house.

15
Regrets

Making news, Sunday 18 May 1997:
A box of 25 Cohiba cigars once belonging to Cuban President Fidel Castro has been sold for US$11,500 at Christie's Auction House.

Comment:
It was a good time for Sally Tully to consider selling her black pearls, although it may be a day or two before she realised this.

"How unfair," muttered Sally to herself between sobs, raising her head from the pillow and feeling totally lost. Two hours had elapsed since Brian's phone call giving her the news of Vincent's death. Two hours in which she had been lying on the bed crying as she had never cried before, and with no one to console her. She couldn't get Vincent's death out of her mind, and she believed it was in some way her own fault for having wanted him so much. Thoughts tumbled through her head, repeating themselves over and over again.

If only she had told Rod she had seen him with Ilma, or told Ilma she had seen her with Rod, than maybe one of them may have regained their senses and none of this would have happened. And why hadn't she? Was it because she was really unsure of what she had seen going on between them at the Post Office, or was it because she wanted Ilma to be having an affair and had therefore purposely done nothing to discourage it?

And the elation she had felt when she heard what happened in the exhibition foyer. Oh, what selfish, selfish elation. The thought it might open the door for her to a more satisfying relationship to Vincent. Why oh why had she not taken her chance then, and followed Vincent home. And why hadn't she done so anyway for Vincent's sake, just to comfort him, to divert him from such a terrible decision. So what did his suicide really mean? Could it be all her dreams have only been delusions, and her belief she and Vincent would possibly at some time be 'as one' was just wishful thinking. Could it be he would never have been anything other than a friend, no matter what the circumstances? And yet she cannot believe it would be possible for her to feel so empty if it were so.

Slowly the sobs receded and she began to move, pulling her body upright and swinging her legs to the floor. She sat on the bed edge for a while, drawing in deep breaths and desperately trying to regain her equilibrium. She told herself she had to go on living, but the emptiness within her persists. Eventually she remembered she had been preparing a cake when Brian had phoned, and the oven would still be on. Instinctively she reacted. Like a robot she walked through to the kitchen and felt the heat coming from the oven and saw the 'ready to use' light on, and the cake standing on the kitchen bench, ready for baking. Automatically she put the cake into the oven and then washed a mixing bowl, and all the time she was thinking about Vincent. She went to put the bowl onto a drying rack, but it slipped through her fingers and crashed to the floor. She slumped down beside the broken pieces and cried again.

"What a meaningless thing to do," she thought. "Vincent is dead, and I'm baking a cake."

And this is how the rest of her day went – doing other meaningless things, crying, and thinking of Vincent, and with just enough sanity left in her to take a double dose of sleeping tablets before crawling into bed.

Ilma was still in theatre when Jan arrived at the hospital. Jan was told it will be several hours before she will be ready to see visitors. Jan left the things which she had brought for Ilma on the bedside locker – including a huge bunch of flowers and a get well card. In the card she wrote she will be back the next day, and then added her telephone number. She talked for a while with one of the nurses, who told her Ilma would recover from her injuries, but she was likely to stay in hospital for several weeks. There seemed little point in hanging around, so Jan departed for home.

On the way back, Jan did a little detour to Dareboolah to see if Nardia was at the gallery. She found Nardia had only just arrived and was getting ready to hang some new paintings. Jan told Nardia of Ilma's accident, and gave her the hospital telephone number. She didn't mention anything about Ilma's affair with Rod.

The gallery was empty of viewers and Jan volunteered to help hang the paintings. It as the first time they had time to say more than a few words to each other, and Jan was surprised at how much they had in common. When they finish hanging the paintings, they continued to chat over coffee.

When Jan eventually got home, Brian had made several necessary phone calls, and was sitting with a glass of wine in his hand. He put down the glass and got up as she entered. "I have some bad news for you dear," he said.

★

Making news, Monday 19 May 1997:
The American Medical Association today published a report supporting the proposed ban on 'partial-birth' abortions.

Comment:
There was no abortion clinic in Sandhaven Creek, a Catholic Church view of abortion prevails. Young ladies requiring this service usually seek it in a larger township, and pretend at the time to be away visiting an aunt. Since vilification in a small closed community could easily backfire, this little white lie was hardly ever challenged.

On Monday morning Ilma awoke. It was only just daylight and for a moment her surroundings puzzled her. She attempted to sit up and found she didn't have enough strength, and any movement causes her considerable pain. Then she realisesd where she was and what had happened.

She looked around, she was in a private ward and there was no sign of any nurses. She saw the flowers and was able to reach the card standing beside them. "Good old Jan," she thought. "A true friend when needed."

A nurse appeared at the doorway and walked towards her. She was given assurance, made comfortable, and provided with pain killers. She slept, and awoke again a few hours later. It was then she learnt of Vincent's suicide.

Ilma experienced a sense of numbness and she was beyond crying. There was a great sadness within her, and it would be a long time before she could analyse her emotions and resolve her guilt. But the news of Vincent's death pushed any feelings for Rod aside, as she came to understand how very much she would miss Vincent, and how lucky she had been to be his wife.

Fondly, and with silent tears, she thought, "You silly goose, Vince, so proud, how typical of you to leave the house and garden so tidy. You silly, silly goose, we could have made up, we could have."

★

On the morning after Vincent's funeral, Sally made a decision to leave Sandhaven Creek. When she awoke late, she laid in bed thinking about it for quite a while before reaching for the telephone and dialing her office number. "It's Sally here," she said. "Can you put me through to the Boss."

Sally told her Boss about her plans for the future and apologised for giving him so little notice. But she did not tell him the real reason for her leaving.

She invited Brian and Jan and a few other close friends out to dinner. But she didn't say anything to them about her feelings for Vincent. She explained her pending departure, telling them she had been given an opportunity to join a refugee aid group based in Brisbane, and was looking forward to doing some overseas field work with them after a suitable training period.

The week after the dinner party, Sally left Sandhaven Creek forever.

16
A Well Respected Citizen

Making news, Tuesday 24 June 1997:
The Australian Minister for Foreign Affairs, Alexander Downer, today announced his intention to visit Athens on Friday. In a press statement, Mr. Downer noted Australia's significant relationship with Greece.

Comment:
The father of Chris Demitrious was one of only a few Greek migrants to open a business in a country town. Most preferred to live and work in the big cities.

Nearly a month had passed and Brian was sitting in his office early on a Tuesday morning. Maureen O'Donavan came in, closing the door quietly behind her. "Joe Bernaldo is here," she announced. "He wants to know if you can spare him a few minutes" Brian agreed and asked her to show him in. Maureen opened the door and within a moment is ushering Joe in. Brian got to his feet.

"Come in, Joe, nice to see you. Have a seat. Would you like some coffee?"

"No thanks, Brian, I can't stay long, it's distribution day. I just thought you might like to be first to have a copy of today's Journal. Something you should see on page fourteen. I was asked not to tell anyone about it until after its publication."

Brian picked up a copy and flicked through the pages. Joe watched him and asked, "How is Ilma? Is she out of hospital yet?"

"She came home on Friday. She's staying at Dareboolah for a while, it's closer to the hospital. She has to go back there for physiotherapy three times a week."

"Is anyone looking after her?"

"Jan's been staying with her, sleeping on a camp bed, it's only a studio apartment. So I don't think she'll stay many more nights, and anyway, Ilma seems to be managing quite well. She can dress herself and make a simple meal, and she has Nardia who looks after the gallery, nearby if she needs anything."

"How does she get to the hospital?"

"Well, funny as it may seem, she's become friendly with Beryl Thomas, the woman she thought was going out with Rod. Beryl found out about the accident and visited Ilma at the hospital nearly every day. Beryl has a cousin from Canada staying with her for a while, and helping out at the hotel. It gives Beryl a bit of free time, so she's volunteered to be Ilma's chauffeur for a couple of weeks. Jan tells me Ilma plans to sell up here and move the gallery business to Armidale. And what about you, have you heard from Rod?"

"No, and I don't expect I will. I don't think we'll ever hear of Rod again. Unless he becomes a top journalist. And this is quite likely, if he sticks at it."

"How are you managing without him?"

"Quite odd really. His wife's freelance friend, Diana Pouchay, who's here doing some research, came to ask me some questions. I talked her into helping out until I can get someone else. This time I'm advertising through an agency and they'll check out the applicants before I see them. Some old dogs can learn new tricks, you know."

Brian laughed. Then, in a more serious tone, he said, "Yes Joe, and talking about tricks, I've been thinking about the photos young Phillip Jackson took when Florian blundered in on Rod and Ilma, You had them destroyed, didn't you?"

Joe sighed. "Of course I did. I told Phillip we look after each other in this town, and so we wouldn't be publishing them. I let him know he would get no more work from the Journal unless he handed over the film. I destroyed it personally, in front of him. And I told him he would understand one day. He's a good lad, he didn't intend any harm."

Joe paused as he got to his feet and stood at the window. He glanced out towards the Journal building, and then he turned his gaze back to Brian. "Life also plays tricks," he said, quietly. "I was in Brisbane when those condemning photos were taken, and I didn't hear about Vincent's suicide, or about the Town Hall fiasco, until the Monday morning. If I had known about the photos in time, I would have assured Vincent they would not be published. As it is, he must have ended his life convinced he would be front page news in the next edition."

For a moment Joe stood there, feet apart and head slightly down. Still looking at Brian he said, "There are times when I hate being a journalist, and this is one of them. I will always wonder if it was Vincent's love for Ilma or his fear of public ridicule which lead him to take his own life."

Realising Brian had reached the article he wished him to read, Joe leaned over the desk and tapped the opened page with his finger. "There it is," he said, straightening up. "I'll leave you to read it. You never know about people. You may be surprised at the end."

Brian walked around the desk and then grasped Joe's hand. "Thanks Joe, for telling me about the photos. I guess I know what you are thinking. Just remember, Vincent was a proud man, but he was also in love with Ilma, and you couldn't have changed anything."

Joe said goodbye, and Brian returned to sit at his desk. He reflected on events for a few minutes before reading the article.

Sandhaven and District Journal - Obituary Column
Tuesday 30th April 1997

A WELL RESPECTED CITIZEN

Sandhaven Creek Primary School Headmaster and Sandhaven Creek Citizens Social Club President, Vincent Rowan Mathews, died suddenly on the 13th of March this year. He was 46.

Vincent was one of Sandhaven Creek's best-known citizens and a tireless worker for the community. Born and brought up in the township, he attended as a child the school at which he was later to become a most popular Headmaster.

Vincent matriculated at Sandhaven Creek High School and went on to take a Bachelor of Education at Brisbane's Top End University. His initial teaching appointment was to an inner Brisbane suburban school, where he stayed for one year before successfully applying for a junior teaching position at his old primary school. Over a span of five years he taught at various levels within the school and was appointed it's Headmaster at the age of 37.

Vincent believed in teaching through example, and he always insisted both staff and students accepted responsibility for their actions, and he personally conducted himself in this way throughout his life. His teaching philosophy, he used to say, was to treat each child as if they were a friend and to talk to each child at their level of understanding.

Vincent became President at the Sandhaven Creek Citizens Social Club in 1991 and would have completed his five-year term of office later this year. His drive and enthusiasm achieved a substantial increase in club membership, and under his guidance the club premises were extended to include the present, very attractive, dining facilities. His calling at the bingo game was a regular club feature, and his ability at the dartboard feared most opponents.

In carrying out his duties as Club President, and in his position of Headmaster at the school, he was well supported by his wife, Ilma. Vincent and Ilma met while she was still at primary school and he was in high school, and their relationship blossomed when Ilma returned to Sandhaven Creek after attending University. Vincent's absolute devotion to his wife was a talking point amongst his friends.

Vincent loved this township and was conscious of most of its achievements and some of its failures. He thought well of its citizens and he wanted them to think well of him. He was a proud man, perhaps sometimes too proud for his own good, but never too proud to listen to people in need.

Vincent will be remembered for his generosity, and for the hard work he undertook in the community's interest.

He will be sadly missed.

-Written by Sally Tully, a friend-

"So now I know why Sally left town so suddenly," Brian muttered, reaching for the phone to talk to Jan.

★

Making news, Wednesday 25th June:
The winning numbers for the United Kingdom National Lottery no.157 are announced: 12, 17, 27, 28, 38 and 40, with bonus ball 6. Three winners share the jackpot prize of £5,000001.

Comment:
Life goes on.

17
Eased Consciences

Making news, Thursday 3 January 2008:
The sighting of a rare none pigmented penguin has excited researchers near Mawson Huts in Antarctica.

Comment:
There was a sighting of a rare bird in Melbourne.

Over ten years had elapsed and Florian had long since sobered up. He had not had a drink since he heard of Vincent's suicide, and realised the part he himself had played in it. He could not escape a feeling of guilt over the unhappy events of that weekend. Nor was he able to remain living in Sandhaven Creek, for he found himself imagining hostility on every face, and in particular, on those of his one time friends.

Within weeks he decided to move to Tamworth.

Sobering up was hard going for Florian, but the rewards had been worthwhile. It wasn't long before he recognised just how bad his paintings had become, and he set about destroying those he had produced while in his alcoholic state, a condition which had lasted for several years. He gained new vigour and threw himself into improving his painting technique, and he gradually began to produce some very good work, which sold well at galleries in Tamworth and Brisbane.

In 2002 he purchased an old bank building with comfortable first floor accommodation. He stripped all the bank fittings and partitions from the ground floor and turned the space into a good-sized studio.

Things went well for Florian until late in 2006 when his eyesight began to fail. His near sight blurred and he became unable to accurately place the point of his paintbrush on the spot he intended. He soon gave up on his last painting attempt, and decided he needed help. He went to his local doctor who diagnosed macular degeneration in both eyes, and arranged for Florian to see a Melbourne eye specialist.

At eight thirty in the morning, Florian was sitting in his studio awaiting a taxi to take him to the airport. He was aware there is no cure for his ailment, and he knew the eye specialist's advice would only be about managing the condition.

Florian had thought about this and came to terms with it. He had decided he couldn't paint again, but he would be able to teach others. He looked around the studio and thought he would be able to accommodate up to six student painters at any one time. He began to plan in his mind just how to re-arrange the studio.

His thoughts were interrupted with the arrival of a taxi. He picked up an overnight bag and opened the studio door. He found it was already hot outside. He hoped his Melbourne hotel room air conditioner would be working. The hotel was on the city edge and he wondered if he should have selected a more expensive one.

In Melbourne, at three o'clock in the afternoon the temperature was 30 degrees and still rising. The eye specialist's rooms were in Collins Street, in the city centre. The air was still and the pavement and the city building's walls were warm to the touch. Florian could feel the perspiration dampening his shirt.

Being unfamiliar with a city the size of Melbourne, and being slightly in awe of it, he had allowed himself too much time to get to Collins Street. He was now very close to the specialist's rooms, but he was a full hour too early for his appointment. He decided to stop the taxi and explore the shop windows. He was not in good condition and started to tire.

Florian founnd himself under the shade of a coffee shop sun canopy. He stopped walking, glanced again at his watch just to be sure, and then sat down at a pavement table. He ordered a long iced coffee, and relaxed.

He was a little bit surprised to find the trees in Collins Street had survived despite all the traffic fumes. Across the road he saw a vacant bench seat. It was in the shade of a tree and almost in front of an ice-cream shop.

As he watched, a slender, youngish looking woman came out from the shop and sat on the seat. She was wearing high-heeled sandals, deep blue shorts, and a light blue sleeveless top. With an ice-cream in her hand, she put a small strap bag down on the seat beside her. She adjusted her sunglasses, moving them from eyes to over her head, and even with his poor eyesight Florian can tell it is Ilma. Her dress style, her demeanour, and her youthful figure are all as he remembered them.

Florian felt he does not wish to meet up with Ilma, but he was happy to sit and look at her. He had no worries about her recognising him if she looked his way. His own appearance had changed considerably. He was now much slimmer, had grown a beard, had an expensive panama hat on his head and was wearing a formal lightweight suit bought specially for his visit to Melbourne.

He continued to sit and watch her, and within a few minutes he saw the ice-cream shop door open again. A young boy of nine or ten years appears. He was slender, with dark hair and olive skin, and he walked gracefully. He too had an ice-cream, a much bigger one.

The boy went over to Ilma and sat on the seat beside her. She gave him a kiss on the cheek and put her free arm around him. They sat there, licking their ice-creams, obviously enjoying the day together.

Florian remembered the last time he saw Ilma, and he found himself more at ease with his conscience. Five minutes later, he paid for his coffee and proceeded on his way to the eye specialist.

End

About the Author

Born in Liverpool, England, Fred Wyke migrated to Australia in 1952. He is an exhibiting solo artist and retired architect who now lives on the Mornington Peninsula.

After working as the first government appointed architect in Alice Springs in the 1950s, Fred moved to Melbourne where he began a short career in politics In the early seventies Fred went on to be elected Deputy 'State' Convenor of the then Australia Party.

Fred commenced writing about ten years ago and has since written two unpublished novels and twenty short stories – some of which have received high commendation in national competitions.

A Tittle-Tattle Town

Fred Wyke

ISBN 9781922175960		Qty
RRP	AU$24.99	.....
Postage within Australia	AU$5.00	.....
	TOTAL★ $_____	

★ All prices include GST

Name:...

Address: ....

....

Phone:..

Email: ....

Payment: ❑ Money Order ❑ Cheque ❑ MasterCard ❑Visa

Cardholder's Name:...

Credit Card Number: ....

Signature:..

Expiry Date: ....

Allow 7 days for delivery.

Payment to: Marzocco Consultancy (ABN 14 067 257 390)
PO Box 12544
A'Beckett Street, Melbourne, 8006
Victoria, Australia
admin@brolgapublishing.com.au

www.ingramcontent.com/pod-product-compliance
Lightning Source LLC
Chambersburg PA
CBHW071301250626
47159CB00004B/1264